THE WOMAN AT THE WINDOW

The Woman at the Window

PADRAIC O CONAIRE

TRANSLATED FROM THE IRISH
BY
EAMONN O NEILL

THE MERCIER PRESS

Mercier Press
www.mercierpress.ie

First published by the Talbot Press in 1921

This edition published by Mercier Press in 1966

This edition © Mercier Press 1966

ISBN 978 1 78117 856 0

Transferred to digital print on demand in 2023.

Contents

The Woman at the Window 7
The Devil and O'Flaherty 29
Put to the Rack 34
As I lay in Bed 48
Little Marcus's Nora 53
Disillusioned 68
The Woman on whom God laid His Hand 81

The Woman at the Window

There was no light in the room save that which came through the window from the street-lamp that stood at the corner of the house. A woman stood inside watering the plants in the boxes on the window-sill and on a little table just inside. She paid particular attention to a pot of fragrant musk with its yellow flowers, but she did not overlook the fuchsia nor the bachelors' buttons. Now and again she looked across the narrow street at the house opposite. Through a window which was on a level with the window from which she looked, but which was without blind or curtain, she saw a young man, apparently not more than eighteen years old, seated at a table covered with books and papers. There were stones on the table also, and, from time to time, the young man would break off a piece of stone with a small hammer and set himself to examine it closely.

A big black cat walked across the woman's room, with his tail erect and jumped on a chair near her.

'You have given me a start, you black thief!' said she.

She sat down at the window. The black cat leaped on her shoulder and began to purr, but her mind was neither on the cat, nor the musk plant, but on the house opposite. The young man was bent over his books and scrutinising the fragments of stone, but the woman was paying no heed to him either. She was looking at the men who had just been working at the outside of the opposite house. They had a ladder against the wall and a man was on top of it. They had affixed a new signboard on the house and they were looking to see whether it had been erected properly. The old signboard, which they had taken down, was leaning against the wall. The woman at the window read the name on it:

```
MICHAEL KIRWAN,

CORN MERCHANT
```

A woman, dressed in widow's weeds, came out of the opposite house and looked sharply at the new signboard. She seemed to be satisfied with it. The new signboard bore her own name. Her husband's was the name on the old one. The old board was pitched into a cart which was driven down the street.

The woman at the window did not leave it. She was tired. She had been busy during the day. She had a good business – a business most helpful to her neighbours. When people were hard up in Three Water Town, when they had to tell the bad old story of want of work and lack of money, food and all necessaries, she was kept very busy. She assisted them all and the man who had a good shirt on his back, or the woman whose boots were not too worn, need never have wanted money as long as she was in the town.

Was she a generous woman? No, but she was an honest woman who had little printed tickets setting out in black and white and red what the person who sought help from her would have to pay. In France she would be called *Ma tante*, and the English would call her *My uncle*. In Three Water Town she was called nothing but Nell. Anyone looking for her could not go astray, for he could see the three brass balls above her door.

Nell herself remained at the window looking over at

the Kirwan's house and at the young man bent over his books and at the new signboard. The fragrant smell of musk was in her nostrils, the black cat, or 'the black thief,' as she called him, was purring on her shoulder, but she was absorbed in thought.

Every night for nineteen years she had sat at this window looking across at Kirwan's and at the old signboard on the wall and to-night, when it was no longer there, she thought that a great change had come upon the world. Old memories came to her unbidden. At first these memories were without shape or form like a mist floating in the air, but gradually they became more clear and coherent and at length they became vivid living pictures before her eyes coming and going ceaselessly.

She no longer saw the house opposite; she no longer saw the student with his books and specimens; she did not see the new signboard with the widow Kirwan's name on it, although it was that which had set her thoughts in train. She had a picture before her eyes. She saw a young graceful man with two grey eyes – humorous, mocking grey eyes. He passes the shop window, just where she is looking out. He stands; he looks at the goods in the window; he sees the young woman.

What a long stretch of time is nineteen years!

She got up from the window and went to the door of the room. She took down a photograph that was hanging on the wall and looked closely at it by the light from the street. She sighed. It was a photograph of herself when she was seventeen. Although the photograph was an old faded one, no previous acquaintance with Nell was required to recognise that she had been pretty then and a surmise that the young man with the grey humorous eyes would appear upon the scene again would not have been far wrong.

9

And he did appear. Did not Nell see him now, although nineteen years had come and gone? She saw him even now, although it was at the young student bent over his books that she gazed.

He had come in one day on which she was in charge of the shop. How her heart fluttered when she saw him! His coming was unexpected.

He placed a watch on the counter.

'How much?' he said, and these were the first words she heard him utter.

She told him what she would advance.

'What is your name?' said she, with her pen in hand.

'Michael Kirwan.'

She wrote it on a little ticket, and, blushing, she handed him the money and the ticket. He made some excuse about his father not having sent him money in time, but his eyes were so bright and mocking that the girl thought that his pockets were full of money.

Who was he? Who was the father who had failed to send him money in time? What was he doing in Three Water Town? Such were the questions that she asked herself after his departure. It had occured to her first that he had come to see her, but she only laughed at the thought. His voice pleased her. And his two keen grey humorous eyes! And his curly hair! She hoped that he would come again; she hoped that his father would send the money so that he might redeem the watch. She thought it would be a great shame if he were to lose it, but she need have had no fear on that score. He came and he came again and, by a strange coincidence, she was always in the shop when he came.

They met often after that at the early Mass on Sundays in St. John's, or in the street when she went shopping, or she saw him in his own boat when she and her father went on the lake for a row on Sundays. In the month of May the Rosary was said in the church every evening. He was there the second night. How did he know that she went there also? To make a long story short, she became very intimate with Michael Kirwan.

The young student in the house opposite with the new signboard got up from the table, stretched his arms and looked towards the window. Nell started. How like his father he was!

Although her eyes seemed fixed upon her musk-plant with its yellow flowers, Nell's thoughts went back to that day on which she had gone for a row on the lake with the father of the young student now stretching his arms in the room opposite. It had been a fine sunny day in the beginning of summer. The countryside was in bloom and the lake lay around them like a silver mirror. The boat moved gently through the water – he rowing and she steering. With every pull of the oars he bent back as if he were leaving her. The return pull brought him nearer to her again, and both of them laughed in the intimate way of people who have a perfect understanding about something. And they did understand each other. They felt that youth was splendid and that it was the only real wealth. As they returned home that evening...

When her recollection had reached this stage the woman at the window got up and spoke aloud.

'Would your father agree?' said she.

'Yes,' I answered.

'And you agree too?'

'How you mock me!' said I.

She sat down again by the window. 'And he married Brigid Ruane though I and my people were awaiting him in the church!' said she, bitterly. 'Brigid was to blame. She stole him from me. But, Brigid!...' Nell got up and shook her hand at the house opposite and at the young student. 'But may I not die, Brigid!...

She checked herself as she saw Brigid Ruane – the widow Kirwan – in the room opposite speaking to the young man. He put away his books and specimens. The look the student gave his mother pierced the heart of the woman opposite like a sharp knife. His mother kissed him (she had begun to do so since her widowhood) and retired to rest.

Nell remained at her own window. The old memories which had been crowding in upon her for two hours, vanished like the water in a shallow pool before the wind, but they came back in a different form more overwhelming and oppressive than before. They were no longer reveries but thoughts – thoughts heavy with sorrow and with hate and the hate was gaining the upper hand of the sorrow every minute. She could not get rid of the feeling of hate, she could not escape from it, and this hate begot feelings of vengeance. This feeling of vengeance appeared to her to be almost a physical reality – a more tremendous, terrible and ugly thing than the hatred from which it sprung. She felt it to be a living, hostile force and she rose up with a start to combat it. She stretched out her hands to keep back the new enemy and a struggle ensued. She ran from the room and went and threw herself on her knees before a little altar which stood in her bedroom. She spoke no word, but as she swayed to and fro before the altar she was herself a living supplication.

She had crushed the enemy, so she thought, but she awoke her old servant, Kate, with her impassioned sobbing.

Next morning Nell opened the shop as usual at half-past seven. Only occasionally did anyone come in so early and anyone who did come was asked by Kate to wait until the return of her mistress from the eight o'clock Mass. This morning, however, the shop had scarcely been opened when Nell saw a bare-footed woman crossing the street. She was a small, timidlooking woman with terror in her eyes. Her gait, her weak mouth, and her keen, rapid glance gave her the appearance of fear personified. She was one of these wretched women who are often to be seen amongst the poor in the large towns and whose every act appears to be an apology for being alive at all. She carried an infant in her arms.

She laid on the counter a large bundle which she carried in the manner of a person making a sacrificial offering.

Nell would rather have seen the Evil One himself than this woman at that hour of the morning. She had no ill-feeling towards her, but she had to crush the enemy who had attacked her at the window the evening before. The sending of this woman into her before she went to Mass was one of the wiles of that same enemy. She had not thought, on the night before, that this wretched woman's husband might be the means by which she could wreak her vengeance on the Kirwans. This was a terrible drunkard, and if only he and the young student could become companions! See how his father had behaved. If his wife had allowed him would he not have drunk himself to death? The Kirwans had a fondness for drink in their blood, but Brigid would not allow a drop across the threshold.

Nell! Nell! you have not crushed your enemy yet!

Nell opened the bundle that the woman had laid on the counter. The first thing she touched was a long linen robe, very white and very narrow – the robe of a newborn babe. She placed it at one side.

'Is he not working?' asked Nell of the woman.

'Yes, but he has drunk all we had. He was off work for a while. He has been drinking for four days. He has just wakened now and he will pull down the house unless I get him a couple of glasses of whiskey.'

Nell took out of the bundle a couple of shirts – shirts without sleeves and so tiny that they would hardly fit a doll. She placed them on the top of the white robe.

'It's bad company,' said Nell. 'If it were not for bad company he would never drink.'

She took up two little pairs of woollen boots.

'I knitted them myself,' said the little woman. 'See the pretty ribbons I fastened to them to keep them on his feet.'

The infant tried to get hold of them, but could not.

'Bad company,' said Nell, as she placed the boots on top of the other articles.

Just then young Kirwan passed the door.

'Look at that young man,' said Nell. 'He doesn't drink. He doesn't go into bad company.'

Nell put a tiny coat of blue flannel with the other articles – a little coat to keep the cold from baby's smooth soft frgrant skin. Baby tried to grab this too, but his mother prevented him, though it was his own little property.

'If it were not for bad companions I would not have to come to you with these things. Only for them he would be happy going about the country gathering herbs and examining them,' said the small woman in a weak voice.

Nell took up a big white shawl knitted in better days to keep the wind and rain from the infant. Looking out she saw the young student passing the door again.

'There would be small chance of his drinking so heavily if he were in company with that young man,' said Nell. 'Both of them travel about the country – the young man collecting specimens of rocks and that husband of yours gathering herbs.'

Nell could say no more. She had not intended to say so much, but the words escaped in spite of her. The enemy was returning to the attack, and the physical obsession of the night before was upon her again. If the young student were to become a companion of this woman's husband before long both would be in bad company! Before long the student would begin to drink! Before long he would get terribly fond of drink! Before long his mother would have a broken heart – she who had stolen her promised husband!

These were Nell's thoughts, but she only said, 'I suppose you want the same money for these things?'

'The same money,' answered the woman, and as Nell handed her the money she added, 'but it would be hard to get them together again.'

'Leave that to me,' said Nell, 'I'll fix that for you, you will see.'

Nell had not intended to say this. She had no thought of doing what she said, but her enemy was near and was urging her on. He was gaining the upper hand.

'If you do that for me,' said the woman, 'I'll say a prayer for you every day I live.'

When the woman was gone, Nell went into the room at the back of the shop. She was trembling. She was going to put on her cloak to go to eight o'clock Mass as she had done for eighteen years, but, when she took up the cloak to put it on, she closed her lips with a snap, threw down the cloak and went upstairs.

She sat down in the big chair by the window and looked across at Kirwan's. The student was in the room opposite putting his lunch and his geologist's hammer into a bag. His mother was at the door. Nell was pondering deeply as she looked at the pair – the son in the room upstairs and the mother at the door. Whatever her thoughts were they left no traces on her countenance. She appeared to be merely inhaling the scent of the musk. She gave no sign that she was hearkening to the whisperings of the devil.

The Mass bell rang, but Nell did not get up. She snapped her lips together again.

In a moment or two she got up suddenly and, going to the mirror over the fire-place, she looked at herself. She shook her head.

'Oh, I'm too old,' she said to herself, 'he is only eighteen.'

She closed her lips tightly again, and remained a short while standing as if she were listening for something. She made a step forward, paused, and then made another step and went downstairs. She took up the old satin cloak, now grey with age, and the little black hat with the feather sticking up coquettishly and she put them on. She went out into the street. If there were any people in Three Water Town who timed their going to work by seeing Nell passing their doors going to Mass they were late on this morning as they did not see her pass. If, however, they had been at the end of a little street near the lake they would have seen a small dark woman wearing an old weather-beaten cloak and a hat with a feather sticking up coquettishly, and they would have seen, too, this little woman going into the house of the woman who had brought her in the bundle earlier in the morning.

On the evening of the same day when the shop was closed Nell was at the window. She saw two men walking down the street each carrying a bag. One of them was the young student and the other man did not leave him until he reached his own door. The other man was the husband of the woman who had visited the shop in the morning.

When Nell saw these two in company she experienced the feelings of a swimmer who hesitates on the river-bank for fear the water might be too cold, but who does not find it a bit cold when he jumps in. She laughed, and if old Kate was disturbed that night it was not by the sobbing of her mistress.

The enemy had triumphed.

Nell was very fond of goat's milk. Every Sunday in the year she went out after the eleven o'clock Mass and made her way along the road by the lakeside. She wore the old satin cloak and the hat with the proudly nodding plume. When it rained she carried an umbrella and she carried the same umbrella to protect her from the sun. She never spoke to anyone but went right ahead until she reached a small house by the lakeside about two-and-a-half miles from the town. She went in and drank a glass of goat's milk. If the weather was fine she sat outside the cottage and looked for some time at the boats going by. Then she would drink another glass of the milk.

Many of the boats came to land there, and many a glass of goat's milk was drunk in that cottage by the lakeside. Many a glass of 'milk' that was never drawn from a goat was also drunk there, but those who drank this liquid had to be known to the man of the house.

The next Sunday that Nell sat outside the cottage door drinking her second glass of goat's milk she saw two small boats racing each other. Each boat held one man. One of the men was strong and stoutly built. The other was young and slight, but he was a far better oarsman than the other. All the people there were looking at the two men, some thinking that the stout man would win, others that the victory would go to the youth. The youth would have won had he not broken an oar just opposite the cottage.

He put his boat ashore and the other man landed too and they both went into the cottage. Nell knew them. They were young Kirwan and the companion whom she had chosen for him.

The student thought he could get the loan of an oar in the cottage, but there was none to be had.

Both men sat inside near the door. They called for goat's milk. The owner of the cottage knew the stout man well, and if what they got had the colour of milk, it certainly had not the smell of milk. They drank a second glass and the big man drank a third.

Nell did not see them as she was outside, but she heard every word they said.

'If I hadn't broken the oar,' said the young man, 'I would have won the bet.'

'You would, but, bad luck to you! drink another glass. The day is hot.'

'I won't, but did you see the wonderful stone I picked up in the Giant's Cave?'

'A half-glass, have a half-glass and we will be going,' said the big man.

'Look at this stone,' said the student. 'The like of it was never seen before. It is like granite and there appears to be a vein of limestone in it. Look! thousands of years ago this stone was buried deep in the earth.'

'I'm going to have another – the day is hot,' said the big man.

He drank another glass, but Nell could not say whether the student drank the third glass. Even if he did not it was plain enough to her when he came out that he had taken more than enough.

When the big man saw the woman sitting outside the

door, he saluted her as he knew her well.

'Are you going home?' he inquired.

'Yes,' she answered.

'You had better come with us in the boat,' he said.

The three of them got into the boat. The two men rowed and she steered. Her mouth was tightly closed as she gazed at the young man. She had not been in a boat since the day long ago when his father rowed her on the lake before the boy was born. She did not know what possessed her to go with them. She looked at the young man opposite her who drew back from her and then came nearer with every stroke of the oar, and she gazed into his grey eyes. Would they have been so brilliant if he had not drunk something? How he talked! Would he not write a fine book about the rocks of the district? Nell could not help looking at him – was he not right in front of her? Was he not like his father as he drew back and leaned forward with the movement of the oar – the lake lying all round them like a silver mirror! But on that day long ago his father had had no drink taken.

Nell herself seemed almost to be intoxicated, as there was a flame in her eyes, a blush on her cheek and her hat with the gay feather was all on one side.

A shower overtook them before they could land and all three got wet.

'Wasn't I a fool to let you hide my bottle this morning?' said the big man. 'We are wet to the skin now.'

On landing, the student went up to an old boat that lay by the lakeshore. The other two followed him. He lifted up a board at the end of the old boat and disclosed the big man's bottle. The two men had a pull out of it.

The board lay on the ground at Nell's feet. On the lower side she saw some letters that had been cut with a knife. She looked at them closely.

M. K.

N. B.

1888

were the letters on the board. M. K. stood for Michael Kirwan and N. B. for Nell Browne. These letters were carved on the day they spoke of marrying – that day on which the lake lay spread like a silver mirror and youth was pulsing in their veins.

She threw the board into the water and looked at the two as they drank.

The same evening as Nell sat at the window watering her plants she glanced across at Kirwan's. She did not see the young student, but she saw his mother weeping bitterly.

A month had not gone by before Nell received a visit from the student. It was dusk when he arrived and he seemed afraid of being observed.

He took a bracelet out of his pocket.

'I want some money,' he said, 'to buy books.'

Nell looked at the bracelet. It was a valuable one. 'From Michael Kirwan to his wife Brigid' was engraved on the inside.

My mother hadn't the money to give me today,' he went on; 'she had to pay a quarter's rent.'

Nell advanced him £3, though she wouldn't have advanced a penny to anyone else if the article was engraved.

'I'll come to release it in a day or two,' he said.

When the shop was closed the same evening, Nell went upstairs. She sat in a chair at the window. She looked across at Kirwan's and she saw Brigid in the room opposite. Nell put on the bracelet and began to walk to and fro. She was in a state of great agitation. She began to talk to herself. Should he not have given the bracelet to her at first? Would he not have given it to her were it not for you, Brigid Ruane? Does the man who lies beneath the sod know that the bracelet he gave his wife is now on my wrist? If he does know does he mind?

Again she was at the window, and, looking across, she saw the other woman.

'He does know, he does know, Brigid Ruane!' said Nell. 'And he would rather see it with me than on you. Michael Kirwan! Michael Kirwan! would you not have given it to me if she had not bewitched you? Give me a sign, Michael Kirwan! that you would have done it were it not for her. Give me a sign, Michael! darling Michael! and I'll be content. I'll leave your son alone. I'll set him on the right path again, Michael, if you only give me a sign!'

She thought that she felt the bracelet pressing heavily on her wrist. She felt the old house shaking and rocking beneath her.

The big black cat crossed the floor with his tail erect and he rubbed himself against her foot. She started up and almost fainted.

She sat at the window again. There wasn't a soul to be seen in the street. It was getting late. Now and again a man passed by – some sailor going to his ship, or a boatman who had put in at the fall of night. Now and again she looked over at Kirwan's and she saw a woman's face at the window, but the woman on the other side withdrew on seeing her. When Nell looked out again she saw the other woman there looking up and down the street.

At last the two watchers heard a sound of music. It was a man singing and both women looked out. They caught sight of each other, but neither withdrew her head. The sound was coming nearer and nearer and both of them recognised the voice. They saw the young student unsteadily walking from side to side. The woman opposite made the Sign of the Cross and disappeared from the window. Nell remained where she was and she saw the mother and son at the door and the mother trying to coax him in.

And not once a week but every night found these two women looking out for the return of the youth. One of them wore a bracelet; the fragrant odour of musk was in her nostrils; the big cat sat on her shoulder; evil thoughts filled her heart and she hoped that the young man would come home more intoxicated than on the night before. The other woman was as pale as a ghost and she murmured a prayer that her son would soon come home. When the two women caught sight of each other, the mother drew back, but when they heard the singing coming near they both looked and saw the young man making his way along with unsteady steps.

By this time the young man cared little for his books or specimens. By this time, too, the woman with the black cat on her shoulder cared little for the eight o'clock Mass. She went to Mass now only on Sundays.

One night, however, Nell had not the bracelet on. She had gone to the shop to get it and put it on for her usual vigil at the window, but she could not find it. She searched everywhere, but with no success. Although she failed to find the bracelet she found something else – a long knife with one blade broken and she found this knife close to the box where she kept the bracelet during the day. She suspected who had mislaid the knife, and whoever had left the knife behind had stolen the bracelet. She handed the knife to the police and a day or two later the student was arrested.

On the night on which he was arrested, Nell was in a little room at the back of the house seeing whether she had lost anything else. Every article that lay before her in this storeroom could tell its story and could reveal many things concerning the life of the poor in Three Water Town. She had the place turned upside down when the student's mother walked in. Nell was astonished at seeing her. She did not know how she had got in, as she thought that the door was locked. Neither did she know of the arrest of the young man.

The mother fell on her knees before the other woman.

'Oh! don't make a thief of him! Don't make a thief of him before the world,' she pleaded.

'He made a thief of himself,' responded Nell.

'Say nothing against him! Oh! say nothing! It would be shameful to say that he stole it. He didn't steal it! My son never stole anything, but he was ashamed of me when I found the bracelet missing. He was afraid I would think he had sold it. I gave him the money to take to you. I gave it to him three times over, but – but – he drank it. Say that he didn't steal it. Say that you yourself gave it to him. Say anything you like. For God's sake and the Blessed Virgin's! O my son! my son! what a state you are in to-night! And he is only nineteen!'

The distracted mother held the other woman by the dress as if to prevent her from turning away. The other woman looked down on the white agonised face beneath. She closed her lips tightly.

'Your son was old enough, Brigid Ruane, to steal my property.'

'To steal your property,' said the mother. She was about to say 'the bracelet that Michael Kirwan gave me,' but she recollected herself in time.

'Yes, it was my property he stole,' said the other woman. 'Did I not advance him money on it?'

'You did, you did, but I will give you your money.

I'll give it to you over and over again. I'll give you everything I have, only don't send him to prison. Oh! don't, don't, and I will give you all I have, and my blessing too, and I will go begging.'

The other woman tried to get away, but the mother held her in a tight grip. The only light in the room was from a candle and it cast two shadows on the white wall behind them – one of a woman on her knees swaying from side to side, the other of a woman standing as stiff as a stake and looking down on the woman on her knees. The west wind came in from the sea over the harbour and through the streets of the town. It was making merry in the chimney of that big house built in the Spanish style.

'I advanced him money on the bracelet, I gave him money for my own property,' said the woman, who was standing, and her voice was as sharp as the wind: 'but if he who is dead were here to-night, Brigid Ruane, he would tell us that he should have given it to me first and he would tell us that he would have given it to me if you had not cast your spell over him, Brigid Ruane!'

The woman on her knees started and loosened her hold somewhat.

'Your son's heart was deceitful from the beginning, Brigid Ruane,' said the woman who was standing, 'and he did not get it from nowhere. He did not get it from his father, Brigid Ruane! Who stole my man from me when he was about to marry me, Brigid Ruane? Many and many a day for nineteen years have I said to myself that I would never rest easy in my grave until I saw the woman who did that deed on her knees before me before I'd die. Now, Brigid Ruane!'

The mother was about to get up, but she gave one more beseeching glance at the other woman, imploring her to save her son. But the other's lips were tightly closed, and there was no mercy in her glance. The west wind began to whistle in the chimney, and the candle was almost extinguished.

'My little son! my little son!' wailed the mother – a wretched object of pity. 'My son! my little son!' she repeated. 'Don't keep him from me! Don't! Don't keep him from me!'

But the other woman had a heart of stone that night.

'You might as well be talking to the wall,' she said, turning her back.

The other woman looked at her for a moment.

'May the curse of the mothers who lost their sons be upon you! May it follow you in this world and may it meet you in the next,' she cried, and so departed.

The other woman did not move. The west wind from over the sea was whistling and sporting in the chimney. It came down the chimney, swept across the floor through the open door and it put out the candle.

The young man was sentenced to three months' imprisonment. He would have received a heavier sentence only it appeared at the trial that there was no one in the shop when he came with the money to redeem the bracelet, that he saw it on one side, that he took it up without thinking of what he was doing, and that he was afraid to go back with it. Nell had to admit that she herself wore it every night at the window.

But she never wore it again, nor did she wear the dress she had on when the other woman called. The marks of that woman's fingers were upon it.

It rained heavily on the day on which the young man was released from prison. After closing the shop Nell went upstairs and sat at the window, although there was no light in the room but what came from the street-lamp at the corner. The musk-plant gave forth its odour and the black cat was on her shoulder trying to be friendly. She looked across at Kirwan's thinking she would see the student in the room opposite. He was not there. He had gone to a friend's, although his mother sought to keep him at home, but he had promised her that he would not stay away long and that he would not drink a drop.

Nell knew that he would be in the room if he were at home. She put away the big cat. She had a kind of fear that he would start drinking again. Her vengeance had been ample. She had sent the son to prison and had brought the mother on her knees before her. But he couldn't be drinking: perhaps he had gone to bed.

She got up and took the bracelet out of the box where she had placed it when the police restored it to her. She went to the window and looked across, holding the bracelet that grey-eyed Michael Kirwan had given to his wife. She stayed some time at the window looking over. She was in a state of great agitation.

A light appeared in the room opposite. Nell saw the books and papers and specimens which the student had left on the table and which had not been disturbed while he was in prison. She saw, also, Brigid Ruane in the room walking up and down and up and down ceaselessly. She saw her seating herself at the window and looking up and down the street. She saw her white anxious face, but when the woman opposite saw Nell she drew back from the window. And when Nell saw the mother moving back, a sudden desire seized her to go over, to give her back the bracelet and to ask her forgiveness. She did not stir, however, although the hatred in her heart was extinguished.

The town clock began to strike – one, two, three – eleven. Both women counted the strokes and they looked out and neither withdrew her head.

It was raining heavily and the west wind swept through the narrow streets. Bits of stick and paper and other objects were being blown about. Nell saw a piece of orange peel flying past the street lamp. Though her mind was disturbed nothing escaped her notice. There were lights in many other windows in the street, but they were being put out one by one.

The big clock began to strike again – one, two, three – twelve.

Nell pitied the woman opposite. She put the cursed bracelet under her heel to trample on it. She took it up again and ran down to the door to go over to the woman. She stopped and returned to the window. The old enemy was still near her.

The big clock began striking again – one – one stroke, but that single stroke brought terror to the hearts of the women. Both of them prayed that they would soon see the son of the man with the grey humorous eyes who was now in his grave.

The moon came out. The wet street was bright and slippery after the rain.

The clock began to strike again – one, two. Two strokes and the women looked at each other. Two sailors passed up the street. The mother put her head out:

'Did you see my son anywhere?' she asked, but before they had time to answer her she was gone from the window.

The clock began – one, two, three, and the women looked at each other again.

They heard a noise. Both strained their ears to listen. What was it? It was coming nearer and nearer, but it was only the clatter of a car. It passed before the two houses, but the two women saw that the driver was asleep and that the two horses were hastening to get home. It was a distiller's cart.

The clock struck one, two, three, four, and the women looked at each other. They heard a song borne towards them on the wind. The young man came in view walking with unsteady feet. He stopped at the end of the street to let the cart pass. The horses were going at a good pace. He tried to get across the street. He slipped. The women uttered a scream together. The cart rolled over his prostrate body.

They say in Three Water Town that he would be alive still if he had not stepped on a piece of orange peel, but others say that he was disgusted with himself and tired of life. Nell is still to be seen at the window inhaling the scent of the musk with the black cat sitting on her shoulder, but when she looks across the narrow street she sees none of the Kirwans in the house opposite. They all occupy a single grave in St. John's Cemetery.

The Devil and O'Flaherty

'The devil and O'Flaherty couldn't do it; no, they couldn't,' said the old car-man to me when I told him that I had to be in Galway before ten o'clock. 'Why, man, if we had a racehorse, we couldn't do it. You won't catch that train to-night, take my word for it.'

The rain was coming down in torrents and the west wind blew a full gale from the sea. Where there were trees by the roadside the wind made the weirdest music in their bare branches. The full moon was somewhere up in the sky if the astronomers were to be believed, but it was completely hidden from us. I was wet to the skin, tired, weary and hungry. The driver was in no better condition. The horse was just dragging his legs after him and his head bobbed up and down like a child's toy horse. The wind shrieked, making a sound like devils' music. The horse started. The driver jumped down and, slowly as the horse went before, he now went very much slower, as the driver held him by the bridle and tried to coax him forward. I said a lot of things about that horse, about Galway car-men, about the weather, the place and other things, but I fear the printer would be ashamed to read them. The driver, however, paid no attention to what I said. Probably he had heard similar language pretty often before. In any case he went on in his own way, as he did not mount the car again until we had gone a couple of miles of the wet road, muddy and full of ruts.

He was between me and the wind, and from time to time I heard him mutter something. 'The Devil' was what I heard oftenest, but sometimes I caught the words 'The Devil and O'Flaherty.' Though I was swearing under my breath myself, I was becoming interested in the driver's mutterings. 'O'Flaherty!' 'Who was O'Flaherty? What had he to do with the Devil? I thought of every story I had ever heard about devils assuming the form of men. Was O'Flaherty a devil in human form? Where did he live? When? What was his appearance? Did he leave any family? Did they take after the father who begot them, or the mother who bore them?

The sky cleared somewhat. The astronomers were right. The moon came out. The driver had been silent for some time.

'Over there on the top of the cliff he lived,' he said suddenly.

I started.

'Who?' I said. 'The Devil, was it?'

'No, but his heir, O'Flaherty Dubh.'

I put him a few questions and soon he let himself go.

'Over there he lived,' he said, 'till the devil came for him in the end. He was a landlord but, even so, many a hundred pounds did he owe all over the country. God help you, man! If he had a couple of thousand a year itself, he was well able to get through it. Racehorses, gambling, dogs, eating and drinking, music and dancing by day and by night. Women – oh! shut up, man! He scandalised the whole countryside. He did, indeed!'

The driver lit his pipe, and I lit mine, but not without difficulty. The driver seemed willing to continue his story.

'Was he married, did you say?' he said, answering me. 'Didn't I tell you he was? He wasn't much more than twenty when he married an earl's daughter from Munster – a kind, charitable, charming woman – but where's the wife who could live in the same house with a man who had a wife in every village from here to Dublin? After the birth of her fifth son she had to return to Munster. The child had not even been baptized when seven carriages drove up to her to the door one night. O'Flaherty himself was in the first carriage. All the occupants – men and women – were under the influence of drink and were singing ribald songs. She tried to keep them out, but they forced the door. They locked her up in one of the top rooms and then pandemonium reigned downstairs. They say that her heart was broken that night. She had left her husband, but the blessing of the people went with her. It did, indeed.

'I tell you that she brought her sons with her too, but he took them from her again after instituting legal proceedings. And didn't he rear them well, piously, and properly! They never went to school and the teaching they got from their father – well, much good it did them. If their father killed a man without rhyme or reason they applauded the deed and said that never was such a fine deed done in Ireland. It was amazing to see these five young men going mad through the country scaring man and beast. I saw one of them myself – Redmon he was called – being hanged in Galway. He had killed his own brother all over a woman.

'He had nine others at home between sons and daughters. Mind, I don't say that his wife returned. Oh, no! not likely! But he got another wife – what's this her name was? No matter. He had three more sons and two daughters by her. What's the use of talking? People wouldn't have said much, perhaps, were it not that he was a bad man in other respects. He never gave anything in charity, and after a night's feasting it was not to the poor that he gave the leavings next day but to his dogs. My father told me that one morning he went there with a car, and saw the dogs and the poor scrambling for the remnants of the preceding night's banquet. O'Flaherty himself was present enjoying the fun. My father struck him. Were it not that the other man was drunk my father would not have got a month's imprisonment.'

By this time we were approaching the town.

'What was the end of him?' I asked.

'Well, indeed, it's hard to say truly,' he answered, 'for there are many versions of the story, but mine is the true one if it was the truth that Big Jack, the bailiff, told me. As I have already said, he owed thousands throughout the country and there was a law then in force that if a man died in debt his body might be seized. He fell ill. He was not at home when the stroke seized him, but hunting with his sons in the hills. He was taken to a little cottage from which he had evicted the tenants years before. He died very shortly. His sons made a coffin to take him home in and they 'keened' him bitterly. While they were 'keening' a man walked in – apparently a huntsman. He was really a bailiff and his assistants were not far off. He expressed sympathy with the young men. He gave them a drink out of a bottle he had in his pocket. They fell asleep.

'It was night – a terrible night like this. Five young men were asleep on the floor. An old man lay cold and stiff in his coffin. Four others getting ready to carry away the body. Two candles stuck in bottles gave them light. They took hold of the coffin, lifted it and put it on their shoulders. A peal of thunder burst over the mountain cabin and the wind rose. The door was shattered and the lights went out. The body-snatchers trembled. One of the young men stirred and yawned.

' 'Oh! oh! he's alive. He's alive,' said one of the bailiffs.

'They put down the coffin on the floor. They were terror-stricken. They re-lit the candles and took a swig

32

out of the bottle.

' 'Better wait and see will the night clear up,' said one of them.

'They agreed, and all four sat down on the floor around the body. They had another swig out of the bottle. A pack of cards was produced and they began to play.

'The night calmed down. There wasn't the least sound to be heard anywhere save the snoring of the young men in their heavy sleep and the falling of the cards on the coffin-lid. The bailiffs themselves got drowsy and fell asleep one by one. The two candles which were stuck in bottles at the head of the coffin were still lighting. One of the bailiffs moved his hand. The cards were all scattered on the floor except one – the one we call the 'devil's own' – and that one lay, menacing and bright at it seemed – right over the heart of the corpse. Again the bailiff moved his hand. This time it touched the card and the card touched one of the bottles and the bottle and candle were knocked over. An odd, shapeless shadow crossed the white wall. The floor about the coffin was littered with dry grass and chips of wood. In a twinkling the place was ablaze. The bailiffs escaped. O'Flaherty's sons also got away, except one who tried to carry off the body. He was burned alive. The body was burned – the cabin was burned. But the people never believed that this was the way O'Flaherty died. The old charred walls of the cabin are still there to prove that it was the devil himself that came to take home his heir with him.'

We were now in the City of Galway.

'Where will you sleep to-night?' asked the driver.

'I shan't sleep at all, I fear,' said I, and I didn't.

Put to the Rack

Next month in the City of Galway a judge and jury will try an action for slander. Burke of Knockmore and Andrew Finnerty are the parties to the dispute and as judgment will have been given before these words are in print, it is no harm to tell the whole story fully.

One day, after his return from America, when Burke was sitting on the ditch where the idlers foregather in the City of Galway, he saw coming up the road towards him a girl who walked with the lightest tread and who had the finest bearing he had ever seen. She appeared to be not more than eighteen, but so dainty were her feet that the marks of her footsteps on the muddy street seemed to be those of a child of twelve.

Burke fell in love with the girl of the tiny feet as she passed him by humming an air to herself. He had a piece of chewing gum in his mouth, but he ejected it through a gap in his upper teeth and it feel circling into the water.

'Who is that young woman?' said he to a hulk of a fellow who sat on the ditch.

'What woman?'

'The little light-footed woman.'

'She is a daughter of Andrew Finnerty's, who keeps the shop near the dock.'

'Andrew Finnerty?' repeated Burke with deliberation. 'Is he a tall dark man?' he inquired, suddenly.

'He is.'

'And has he a mole under his left ear?'

'He has, indeed, and a big one too.'

'And has he lost the top of his right thumb?'

'You know all about him, it seems.'

Burke jumped off the ditch, seized his umbrella, and made off at top speed. He crossed the bridge in a great hurry and never cried halt until he reached the dock.

Finnerty's shop was stocked mostly with boating gear, and the stranger paused a bit outside looking at the shop and trying to think what he had best buy in such a place.

He walked in.

'Sixpence worth of mackerel hooks,' he said.

The proprietor himself was present and he handed them to him.

'Isn't it queer that you don't know your old friend? What a bad memory you have!' said Burke.

The shopkeeper scrutinised closely.

'It can't be that you are James Burke – you are very like him.'

'I'm the same man.'

Finnerty gave him a hearty welcome. They had not met for twenty-seven years, since both were working together in the States.

The stranger was invited into the room behind the shop. The two old comrades sat down, glasses were filled, and they began to chat.

'How long is it since we were in Panama?' asked the shopkeeper.

'Twenty-seven years this Christmas.'

'And I suppose you got married?'

'I didn't. I never had time.'

'I suppose you have made a tidy bit of money, James?'

'I have some.'

They heard a sailor in the shop asking for a couple of fathoms of cord. The shopkeeper went to the door, told him to sit down and said he would not keep him long. He filled the glasses again.

'As for you,' said Burke, 'I needn't ask you.'

'No. I'm a widower with a houseful of children. All daughters, except one son.'

'Do you say so?'

The sailor in the shop was getting impatient and the shopkeeper had to go out and serve him. When he had gone, Burke began to think. Why should he go away again? Hadn't he made enough money? Wasn't a rest good after such strenuous work? And where could he find a nicer place to spend the rest of his life in than the place where he was born? When leaving the States he had intended to pay only a short visit to Ireland, but as the days and the months slipped by his desire to return became less and less. The old enchantment! The old call of the blood!

When Finnerty came back from the shop his friend said to him –

'I came home to get married, Andrew! I am tired of the life over there.'

'One of the Blakes has a fine farm for sale over at Knockmore, if you know the place. You'd get it for a thousand pounds. He wants twelve hundred, and there is as fine a house on it as you ever saw.'

'Have you a car?'

'I have.'

'Yoke the horse at once, and let us go and look at it.'

While the horse was being harnessed, they spoke as follows:

'You have a very bad memory, Andrew!' said Burke. 'Don't you remember the Christmas night long ago when we gave our word that one of us wouldn't want for a wife so long as the other had a daughter?'

'I do remember it, and I'll keep my promise if what you tell me about the money is true.'

'If she herself is willing.'

'Why shouldn't she be?'

'Women nowadays are astonishing. Look at them in England. There's no limit to what they'll do.'

Before the car reached the door the match was agreed upon.

A few nights afterwards Mary Finnerty and her father were together. He told her about the match. She was not satisfied with her proposed husband and said she would never marry him. Her father insisted that she should. Mary swore that she would not.

All the same they were married.

It is true that they had a fine house in Knockmore and everything in keeping with it. The house had been built for a gentleman, but in the course of time he became impoverished, and he had to sell out and go away. No wonder the people thought it a fine match for Miss Finnerty. What had the Finnertys ever had even at their best? And even if her husband was getting on in years, who would realise that he was nearing fifty? Was there a young man in the Parish of Knockmore who could work like him? Where was there anyone with the same 'go' in him? Wouldn't it delight your heart to see him working? And he was so fond of her! The insignificant little thing without energy, or health, or anything!

The neighbours were right. He was a vigorous man. He was fond of work, and he was very fond of the little woman he married.

But she was not content, and her dissatisfaction was due to the queer way in which he showed his affection. He was a bit rough. Perhaps this was due to his life in America, to the grinding work there and to all he had seen. Anyway, she trembled a little when he came near her for fear he would prove too loving. A little shudder of goose-flesh passed over her as he touched her.

She would not confess to this feeling for anything in the world. She thought it would be a great sin to do so, but, nevertheless, she was pleased in spite of herself when he told her that he was going to such and such a fair and would be away for a few days. She could not help her feelings. She could not possibly love him in the way a woman loves a man, and as soon as he had departed she tried to find out whether many women of her acquaintance were in a similar plight.

He did not understand how matters were with her. He was clever, intelligent and vigorous-minded. In a bargain he would certainly not come off second best. He was well-informed in business matters and on political questions, but he failed to understand people who had not his own rough outlook. What was the cause of this? His life in the States, his incessant labour, his strenuous existence, and the scramble for money? Or was it a natural warp in his temperament?

Often when his wife was discontented and out of sorts, and when an appropriate word would have made her all right, he would say something rough that would make her worse. He often noticed her in this way, but he did not understand the cause of it. He had never met a woman like that before. The women whom he had come across in the big cities of America liked nothing better than flattery and presents.

He resolved to give his wife a beautiful present in the hope that it would dispel her queer moods. He went to Galway for the sole purpose of buying this present. He visited all the shops and he finally decided on a fine dress of glacé silk made in the latest fashion. In addition he bought her a large gold brooch. He was always most generous to her, but in the purchase of these articles he went somewhat beyond measure. It was of no consequence, however. Wouldn't she be delighted when she saw them?

And she was delighted. She had never seen such a lovely dress and its style was perfect. When her husband held it up to show it to her it seemed so dainty that it would not fit even the most slender woman.

His wife took it to put it on.

'I am most grateful to you, James! Most grateful indeed,' said she.

She put on the dress and it was too small for her. He told her so.

'I'd prefer it that way, James! I'll be in the fashion.'

'But in a month or two you won't be able to put it on at all.' He said a great deal more to her that I will not mention. It displeased her and when he would not stop she burst into tears and fled to her own room.

He was sorry for having spoken to her in that way. He knew that she did not like such language and he knocked at the door to go in and apologise to her. She would not let him, however.

'Open the door,' he said.

'I won't,' she answered.

He was getting angry.

'The longer you stay outside the better I'll be pleased,' said she.

She opened the door slightly, and flung out the dress.

'And if you want to give a present in future,' she said, 'give it to somebody else.'

He was very angry. He stood for a few minutes at the door between two minds. He would have liked to put his shoulder to the door, to break it in and to thrash her soundly. He did not do it, however, but he took up the fine dress from the floor and threw it into the fire.

'The devil take her!' he said, 'but I'll teach her manners,' and with that he flung out of the house, rode off on a white horse of his, and never stopped till he reached the town.

He was seen that night on the road swearing terribly and beating his poor horse unmercifully.

When her baby boy was born it never saw the light. Two doctors from Galway were called in, but the child was born dead, and the doctors expressed the opinion that if she had another child she would not survive.

When she got better her husband took practically no notice of her. About this time he commenced going from fair to fair buying cattle to fatten on Knockmore, and often she did not see him or hear from him for a week. She did not mind this in the least. Even when he was at home they spoke but seldom. He got up, ate his break-fast, went out to look after the stock and she would not see him till dinner time. Almost every night he had com-pany in the kitchen and spent a good part of the night playing cards and carousing. He had always drunk a fair share, but he was as strong as a bull and was well able to stand it. But his bad habits were gradually getting the upper hand of him, and it was often daylight before he went to bed. Oftener still he did not speak to his wife for a whole day or two days on end unless to ask her whether she had done this or that, or whether she wanted money for household expenses.

She was of the opinion that he had no longer any respect for her, and where there is no respect there is no love. She was pleased that this was so. She would have been content, or half-content, if he had left her alone except for the necessary few words. She would have a wretched life tied to a man whom she hated, but how could she escape it?

He had bought out his land completely and one night that he came home drunk from the fair of Galway his wife learned something of what was troubling him.

'He won't get it whoever gets it,' said he to himself as he sat by the fire while she got ready the supper.

'He won't get it, the fool, the cursed knave, the rogue!' said he not noticing the presence of his wife.

It was not long until she knew what was in his mind.

'He knows that none of my people are living, but neither he, nor his people will get it. I'd rather sell the land and throw the money into the sea.'

He raised his head and saw his wife. It was very late and she had got up to let him in for fear he might be killed on the flags outside. If he had met his end far from home and unknown to her she would not have cared. When he raised his head and when she looked at him she thought that she had never seen, and hoped that she would never see again, a human face so ugly. She tried to get away from him and go to her own room, but with a coarse remark he caught her by the shoulder.

She succeeded in shaking him off he had so much drink taken, and he fell on to the floor and remained on the cold flags till morning.

He rode the white horse from fair to fair and from town to town, and man and horse were frequently seen travelling the road at midnight – the rider in a drunken sleep and the horse guiding him itself. His wife was at home and any night she expected him she could not sleep till he arrived. She remained up not because of any remnant of affection for him, but she sat at the window listening for the horse's hoofs on the road, hoping she might never hear them and that the rider would drink that last drop that would precipitate him from the saddle on his head on the road.

And visions come before her eyes. She saw her husband being brought home some morning dead. The neighbours would condole with her on the loss of a good husband, and she thought of what she would say to them, or whether she could mourn his loss.

She was, however, a good pious woman, and such thoughts came to her in spite of herself. She never willingly harboured them.

Then she would hear the horse, far away, trotting on the hard road, and she would strain her ears to catch the sound of her husband's voice and to learn from it in what state he was, for she knew how drunk he was by his voice and her terror varied with its sound. When he came home in a maudlin sate and showed her affection in his rough way she tried to elude him, but seldom succeeded. How she hated him! How she loathed him as she felt his heavy drunken breath on her cheek! She was a timid little thing by nature and she would never have taken any steps if it were not for something he said to her one morning at breakfast. He made it clear to her that he had no respect for her and that he could not think much of such a woman – who had not given him an heir.

Before he left the house he said a lot more that troubled her greatly. She saw him go down the road on the white horse, and she prayed that he might never return.

But the same night she was at her post at the window listening for the horse. It did not come. Midnight passed, and one, two and three o'clock and no sign. She had time to think of the wretched life she was leading, but what pained her most was what he had said to her that morning and the manner in which he had said it. It was a bright moonlit night, and a sudden desire seized her to go out.

She left the house, and no sooner was she outside than she resolved never to return. She drew her cloak round her and, setting out to walk to Galway, she did not halt until, before dawn, she stood on her father's hearth.

After three days Burke went to Galway for her. He found Finnerty at home, and he was taken into the room behind the shop.

His glass was filled, as was always done.

'This is a very bad business,' said Finnerty.

'She herself is to blame,' replied Burke.

Her father had heard only part of her story. The young woman had been ashamed to tell him the worst, and even if she had done so he would not have understood aright. He thought that it was nothing but a young woman's whim, and that it could be easily remedied. He had advised her to go back to her husband, but she refused. This was, in his opinion, only youthful nonsense, but he thought it well to teach her husband a lesson and to give him a fright. He had been too long indulging in drink and late hours.

'I suppose you have come for her,' said Finnerty.

'And so she is here?'

He had suspected that she was not.

'Where else would she be? And she says that here she will stay.'

'Not here. I am her husband.'

Burke assumed a bold attitude. Right was on his side, he thought.

'You've been drinking and carousing too much for the past year,' said Finnerty. 'I wouldn't blame a man for taking a drink now and again, but every night in the year! Wherever I go I hear nothing but 'did you hear what Burke of Knockmore did lately?' or 'isn't he a terrible drinker?' It's a shame, man! It's a shame!'

'I don't care a straw what they say. I know my own business best – but where is Mary?'

'You know your own business all right, but my daughter is married to you!'

43

'If they haven't the truth they will tell lies.'

'And the truth is bad enough.'

'Yes,' said Burke in a hesitating tone, as he tried to guess how much of the truth had been told to his old friend.

'Make it up in God's name,' said Finnerty, 'and don't let the world be laughing at us. I'll call her.'

He called her and she came in hurriedly. She bowed to the two men.

'If you have come for me, James!' she said to her husband, 'your journey has been in vain.'

'You will have to come with me. I am your husband.'

'Oughtn't you take advice?' interposed her father. 'However wise you are you cannot understand everything.'

'I was terribly foolish when I gave in to you both at first, but I have bought sense since then, and I have bought it dearly, and you both know that I have had a hard teacher.'

She went on to speak, and the two men were surprised at the vigour and boldness of her remarks.

'Is it go back to that fine house in Knockmore and live there with that man who has insulted me every day – that man who is so coarse that he doesn't even know when he is insulting! The man who never wanted anything but to satisfy his unbridled appetite!'

Her father tried to stop her. He had not thought that things were so bad. If he had known perhaps he would not have advised her to go back.

But now she had put aside all shyness and timidity. She would speak her mind out whatever would be the consequence. The two men were at either side of the table and she stood at the head, but she was so excited that she had, at times, to take hold of a chair to steady herself.

'I would far rather spend my life and my health begging from door to door than spend a single night in the same house with you, James Burke!'

Her father made a quiet remark. He was rather afraid of her.

'And I am far from being grateful to you,' she said to him. 'You only wanted to get me a husband and you didn't care a jot what sort of a man he was so long as he had a little money. To sell me – that is all you wanted. There are some men and God shouldn't give them daughters. There are others and it is a great crime for them to get wives –'

'Stop, woman! Be silent, I say,' shouted Burke in a threatening tone. 'I have only one word to say,' he continued. 'You are my wife, and where I am you are, and unless you come home willingly with me, I'll find other means.'

He attempted to take hold of her, but Finnerty went between them, and for a moment it looked as if there was going to be a struggle.

'You had better go home to-night, Burke!' said her father. 'The matter is not going to be settled in that way.'

Burke went away.

That night two men – one in Galway and one in Knockmore – thought long and deeply on the surprises of woman's soul.

A week afterwards Burke was astonished to get a letter from his wife saying that she was willing to return if he would come for her.

He came and on their return home on the car it occurred to Burke to ask her why she had given in. He was proud that he had brought her to reason.

'There was no use in your tormenting yourself,' he said. 'Didn't you know that you would have to come back? I suppose your father told you that he couldn't keep you at home with his big family.'

'That isn't the reason why I am here with you now,' she answered. 'If he had only a second bit in the house he'd give me one.'

'Why, then, have you given in?'

'Whisper,' she said, and she spoke a word in his ear known only to him and her.

It was nightfall. The old white horse was ambling along in his own way. There was not a breath of air. The birds had ceased their song. The couple on the car heard no sound except that made by the horse and car. One thought was troubling them both. Burke looked at his wife. She was sad and deep in thought, and her hand lay wearily on the well of the car. He put his hand on her hand and stroked it gently, fearing in his heart that she might draw it away. She did not withdraw it.

'Mary! Mary!' he exclaimed, but could say nothing else.

She bore a son, but died at its birth.

. . . .

Some time after this a young man was walking the road near Knockmore when he heard a car behind him. Burke was on the car, and as the young man knew his late wife and her father he gave him a lift. Burke was on for talking and the young man contented himself with listening.

'He'll pay dearly for it,' said Burke. 'The idea of saying that I killed her, considering how fond of her I was! But there is law in the land still, and I'll show him that he cannot call me a murderer.'

They were passing Knockmore Cemetery.

'She is buried there,' said Burke. 'There is her grave. He stopped the horse.

'We may as well go in and say a prayer for her soul.'

The two men knelt over her grave, and when they had prayed for her soul, Burke said:

'I thank you, God! that you did not lay too heavy a hand on me, and even if you have taken away the woman I loved since first I saw her, she has left me an heir.'

A feeling of disgust seized the young man at the thought that the other man did not care what had happened to his wife so long as he had a son, and he let him continue his journey alone.

As I lay in Bed

As I lay in bed last night I beheld a tiny little room, bare of furniture save for a couple of chairs, a table standing beneath a window with broken panes and a low bed capable of holding only a child, or a very small person. An old man was in the room with his fine face clearly marked with signs of sorrow. He wore a corduroy breeches, rough heavy shoes covered with wet mud and a woman's cloak across his shoulders. His hair was long and gray, his head was bowed and he sat quietly opposite the fire beside the lowly pallet. The fire alone made the place visible, for the little tin lamp hanging on the whitewashed wall was not lit.

Someone knocked at the door and two persons entered. The old man neither raised his head nor spoke. The visitors were a very old woman bent in two and a girl apparently not more than seventeen years of age. They kept silence too. They almost seemed not to have observed the old man, but I paid more particular attention to him as I tried to penetrate the cause of his deep grief.

The old woman and the girl moved across the room slowly, and I noticed that the younger woman was leading her companion. They went towards the bed and, on reaching it, the old woman stretched out her brown withered hand, and it rested on the forehead of a young woman who lay there. Was the young woman asleep? I thought so at first, and I continued to think so until the old woman uttered a moan and both of them fell on their knees and began to pray earnestly for the soul of the dead.

48

The sorrow-stricken old man never moved all the time, and he kept silent sitting on the floor with bowed head.

The girl got up and laid upon the body some flowers she had brought with her. The other two paid no heed to her and took no interest in what she did, and this apathy caused me some surprise.

'I preceive the odour of honeysuckle,' said the old man after some time. 'If my daughter were alive –'

' 'Place a little branch of honeysuckle in my coffin,' she said to me yesterday,' said the girl, weeping copiously. 'I left the city early to pluck it.'

Suddenly the old man got up, and, with terrible agitation, moved to and fro across the room. There was no longer grief nor sorrow in his face, but a look of hungry desire as he stooped over the bed and passionately kissed the dead girl. I shall never forget the awful eagerness, the covetousness in his gaze.

'I would give up my share of heaven – of God's heaven – if only I could see you, darling! Treasure! if only I could see you for one moment – for only a moment – O God! O God of Glory! All I want in the world is to see my daughter before I die. Great God of Glory, listen to my prayer!'

After this outburst he squatted on the floor and fell back into silence. I did not notice the departure of the women I was so much absorbed in pity for the blind father.

2

As I lay in bed last night, I heard a music that moved my heart – a music low, sweet, entrancing – a melody that would bring calm to the demented. On opening my eyes

I saw the sorrowful old man sitting on the floor near the bed where lay the body and he had a fiddle in his hand. I was to hear from him no distinct melody, no stream of music, no rushing sound like that of a river, but it seemed to me that the whole room was filled with music, with marvellous, almost inaudible sound, that could never reach a human ear unless evoked by this musician. In it was the soft sound of waves breaking on the beach on a calm summer day: it brought to mind meadows covered with big waving flowers in which sauntered stately women; it induced a desire to sleep, to swoon away into unending gentle repose, but the tranquil face of the musician kept the attention fixed.

He continued playing. I heard the sound of a child's snoring through the music which now was becoming fainter and fainter until at last I heard only the snoring. The player, however, seemed to have it for ever in his ears.

O player, blind player! have you no thought for your daughter, your daughter who lies beside you dead?

3

As I lay in bed last night I heard lively, merry music from the same player – music that would set you dancing and lift all sorrow from your heart. There was, too, such magic in the music that one could not listen to it long without perceiving many marvellous sights coming forward and receding according as the melody altered. In the first of these visions I beheld a broad plain from afar. There were trees here and there waving before the wind. There were many coloured flowers. There were soft white clouds mingling together across the sky and I heard – I am sure I heard – the same merry music wafted towards me on the breeze. When, however, I tried to hear it better I heard nothing at all. The music died away, but the pleasant prospect remained. The beautiful plain was still there and right in the centre of it were two persons – an old woman and a girl – the old man playing music and the girl dancing – dancing happily and merrily, with her long hair floating in the wind.

When I raised my head, I saw nothing but the old man sitting on the floor with his fiddle in his hand. He had not now the old sad look in his face, but had the look I saw in the face of the musician on the beautiful plain. Old man! old man! ought you not be ashamed to be so merry when your daughter is dead?

The old man changed the melody suddenly, and I beheld a long, cold, wet road. The old man and the girl moved along it weary and exhausted. He was querulous and she was leading him by the hand and trying to soothe him by telling him that they had not much farther to walk, that they would be home in an hour, that a good fire and food and comfort awaited them.

O daughter! daughter! why are you telling falsehoods? Do not believe her, old man! Blind musician sitting there on the floor, do not believe her! If you were not blind would you not know that it was on that long, cold, wet road that the horrible thief met her – the ugly thief that snatched her from you? But a father playing music and his daughter lying dead!

4

As I lay in bed last night, I heard the saddest music that I ever heard. A father's grief and a mother's grief were in it, the sorrow of a friend bewailing the loss of a friend, the agony of a sweetheart bereft of his beloved. I put my fingers in my ears, for the sad music was going through me, piercing me to the marrow. I tried to get up and go away but I could not. The old musician held me fixed, and had cast a powerful spell over me. He wished to split my heart in two, and perhaps he would have succeeded if the music had not been suddenly stopped.

Two persons came into the room where the musician was – an old woman bent in two, and a girl leading her by the hand. The old woman was terribly angry.

'We have been listening to you,' said the old woman, 'for half-an-hour, and you should have been on your knees beside that bed rather than playing your music with your daughter dead.'

The old man did not reply, nor did he stir. The fiddle lay on the floor beside him, gripped in his left hand. His right hand rested inertly on the bed and his head lay over on his daughter's body.

When the old woman failed to get an explanation from him, or even a reply, she and the girl departed – the old woman muttering that she would tell the neighbours how little was his grief for his daughter. But when, after their departure, he began to play the mournful music again, I understood him and the meaning of all the music he had played from the beginning became clear to me. I saw that he had not been playing aimlessly nor heartlessly, but that, by means of his music, he had been making a mental picture to himself of the happy time he and his daughter had had together, and of the gloom that would enwrap him now that she was dead.

Musician! blind old musician! I do not pity you to-night when I think of the noble gift you have to bestow on your dead child!

Little Marcus's Nora

You can scarcely imagine how astonished were the people of Rosdaloch when they heard that Little Marcus's Nora was about to go to England. A sister of hers was already working there, but Nora was needed at home. She was going to leave the old couple alone. She had two brothers, but they were wastrels – no good for themselves or to anyone belonging to them. Martin, the elder, had been sent to Galway as a shop-assistant (old Marcus always had big notions), but he was not long there when he lost his position through drink, and he then enlisted in the army. As for Stephen, the second son, the old man had no hope of ever making him a 'gentleman,' but when this wayward youth failed to get his own way from his father, he cleared out, taking with him the price of two bullocks that he had sold at the fair of Oughterard.

'His company is no better than his absence,' said the old man when he heard that he had gone. But he was only pretending that the matter was not worrying him. Many a sleepless night he spent thinking of his two sons who had left him and were going to the bad. If any of the neighbours attempted to console the stubborn old man, or to sympathise with him in his misfortune, he would only say –

'What's the good of people talking? Little thanks I got from them when I tried to keep them in the old nest. They both took wing and have left me alone. I am not going to worry much about them in future.'

But he did worry, and until Nora announced that she had decided to remain at home no longer there was nothing troubling him but the way in which his sons had left him. They had disgraced him. He was the laughing-stock of the countryside – he and his children. And the plans he had made for giving them a good way of living! The way he had worked himself to the bones, early and late, wet and dry, to keep them at school and give them as good an education as the master himself!

But things would be different with Nora: so he thought. He would keep her at home. He would get her married, and after his death she and her husband would have the farm. When she told him that she was going away, he thought at first that she was only joking, but it was soon quite evident that she was in earnest. When he realised the truth, he moved heaven and earth to keep her at home. It was all in vain and the arguments of his wife were no more effective. For a whole month things were in a state of great tension. The old man threatened her with all sorts of ill-luck if she went away, while she tried to reconcile him to her departure. She had determined to go, and go she would no matter what they might say.

'You had two sons,' she said to him one night, 'and they left you. They both disgraced you. There's no knowing but that I may do the same if you don't let me go with good will.'

'She is the last of them all, Marcus!' said his wife, 'and indeed I think it hard to part with her in the end of my days, but,' continued she, almost crying, 'perhaps it is all for the best.'

Her father thought otherwise. He was sure of it. He was quite certain that it would be far better for her to re-main where she was and marry there. After his own death her husband would come in for forty acres of land. She was a gentle, lovable girl. There was not a farmer, or shopkeeper in the seven parishes around who would not be glad to marry her.

'And why not?' said the old man. 'Such a fine girl and forty acres of excellent land!'

But ultimately he was forced to yield.

Then the work began. The intense anxiety which had for some time been weighing upon Nora seemed to have vanished. There was not a trace of it left. She was, or at least appeared to be, as cheerful and buoyant as she had ever been. And she had so much to do! Hats and dresses to be made and fitted! All kinds of stuffs to buy and dye! She had no rest for the week before her departure – visiting here to-day and there to-morrow.

She never shed a tear until the two big portmanteaux she had bought in Galway were hoisted on the car that was to take her to Ballynahinch Station. Then she cried bitterly, and when they reached the cross-roads her tears were falling like rain.

'God help her!' exclaimed a young man who was lying on a mossy bank by the roadside.

'Amen!' answered another man, 'and everyone in her position.'

'But do you know on what pretence she is going away?'

'I shouldn't be a bit surprised if things weren't going on too well at home with her.'

'Three men were looking after her last year – three, too, who had the name of being very well off.'

'I hear that she had a great liking for a son of John Mat's, the shopkeeper,' said an old man who was in the group.

'He who was at college in Galway?'

'Yes.'

'Don't believe it. He was no good.'

'You may say that!'

The car was going north over the great swamp that lies between Ross and Ballynahinch. Nora could still see her own house away down from her in the valley. But it was not of the house she was thinking, but of the unlucky day on which she had first met John Mat's son at the Rosdaloch cross-roads while he was spending a holiday at his uncle's. And that thought did not leave her until they reached Ballynahinch. The train gave a sharp impatient whistle as if to warn people to hurry up and not detain such a big active, powerful thing as it.

Nora got in. The train moved off, travelling very slowly at first. Little Marcus moved along with it. He gave his daughter his blessing and returned home sad and desolate.

2

That wise old man who lay stretched on the mossy bank by the roadside observing the world as it passed by him was right when he said that Nora had once been very fond of John Mat's son. But that time was past, and her feelings now for the smart young man who was studying medicine in Glasgow were those of hatred and loathing. Because of the great liking she had for him, she was now leaving Rosdaloch and her relations and was facing the wide world. Once she had thought more of that rollicking youth who spent his holidays at Rosdaloch than of anyone else she had ever met. What wonderful stories he told her of life in the big cities across the water! How she had enjoyed his conversation! How pleased and delighted was the simple girl when he told her that he had never met anywhere anyone whom she liked better than her! And the splendid house they would have in some great city when he became qualified.

She believed all he had told her, and he believed it too at the time. When he had gone away he never worried, however, about what he had said. It was different with Nora. She longed for his return, longed for the summer, longed for the time when it would be always summer for her.

She believed in him implicitly, but her trust was ill-founded. Her letters were returned by the post office. He had left his address, and no one knew where he had gone. Her life became darkened. Her brain swam like molten lead when she realised the matter fully. She thought and thought about it day and night. There was only one thing to do – leave the place altogether. She had disgraced herself and all belonging to her before the world. A girl who had been a servant in her family at Rosdaloch was working in London. She would go to that city, and thither she was now proceeding and not to the other city where her sister lived.

As she sat in the train she wondered to see rivers, bays, lakes, mountains, and plains sweeping past her and she herself quite idle. Where was she flying from all these things? What kind of life was in store for her in that strange country whither this wonderful conveyance was taking her? She was seized with terror. Darkness was falling over hill and plain. She ceased to think, but now it seemed to her that she was riding on some wild animal; that she heard her heart beating with fright; that the animal was a fiery dragon with flames darting from its eyes; that it was carrying her off to some frightful wilderness – where sun never shone, nor water ever flowed; that she was being compelled to go against her will; that she was being banished to this wilderness for a single sin.

The train reached Dublin. The city seemed to her to be

one tremendous clamour. Men shouted. Trains came and went, whistling loudly. The people, the trains, the cars made a terrible din. She was astonished at everything she saw – the boats and ships in the Liffey, the bridges, the streets still lit up though it was midnight, the people, the city itself so fine, so much alive, so bright at that late hour. She almost forgot for a while the misfortune that had driven her from home.

As she sat in the London train her old worries came back. The dark gloomy thoughts crowded in upon her. She could not put them away. She could not stop them. Why had she left home at all? Had she not better have stayed there no matter what might happen? What would she do now? What was in store for her in the place to which she was going?

Such were her feelings. Nora surpassed the imagination of those folk of old who are said to have lived through long, long years as if they were but a single day. She compressed a hundred years into a single day. She became suddenly old. She experienced every sorrow and every torment and every trouble of mind that comes to one during his whole life in the course of this single day – from the hour she left Rosdaloch until she arrived in London and met Kate Ryan, the servant girl from home, waiting to welcome her on the platform. She had known nothing of the world until that day.

3

The two girls lived in a mean, ugly, back street at the south side of the city. The house was a tremendous size, and the inhabitants were so numerous that they seemed to live on top of one another. Nora was amazed when she saw how many were there. She would have sworn that there were at least a hundred, between men, women and children. She was alone the whole long day, as Kate was out working from morning till evening. She sat at the window looking out on the street at the passers-by and wondering where they were all going. Soon she began to think that she had made a great mistake in coming at all. Why had she left the lonely village among the mountains by the seaside? What would her father say if he knew the reason? He would be furious. 'Why am I so unfortunate compared to other people?' she would say. But the question was insoluble, and when she failed to answer it she went out, but did not go far for fear of getting lost. The crowded streets brought no relief to her worried mind. One night on Kate's return from work she found Nora crying over the fire.

'Now, now, Nora dear!' she said, 'dry your eyes and have a cup of tea with me. I've been told to tell you that a relation of my mistress's wants a servant, and that if you would go –'

'I'll go,' said Nora starting up.

Next morning she went to the lady's house and started work there. She had so much to do and her new experiences were all so fresh that she thought of nothing else for some time. All her letters home contained a little money, even though, when sending it, she knew that they did not need much as they were comfortably off. She read and re-read her father's letters every night before going to bed. They contained news from home – that the herring-fishing had been very good, that Big Pat's Tom had bought a new boat, that Nelly Griffin had gone to America.

A couple of months passed in this way, but, in the end, the lady told her that she was not giving satisfaction, and that she would have to leave. She left, leaving all her belongings behind her. She had nowhere to lay her head that night. She was footsore and wet to the skin.

Need I speak of all that happened to her after this? Of the fine gentleman who gave her food and drink and money when she was at the very end of her resources; of how she learned to drink; of how she tried to woo forgetfulness in drink; of the queer people she met in public-houses and elsewhere; of their conversation; of the way she lost her self-respect and came not to care what happened to her; of the way in which she went from bad to worse from day to day, losing her honour and winding up on the streets?

4

Nine years she spent this way – drinking and carousing at night, tricking herself out in the daytime in preparation for the coming night. She speedily banished from her mind any stray thought that came to her about the life she was living, or the life she had lived at home. Such thoughts caused her the greatest pain. She was forced to put them to flight, for no one can go on living unless he believes that, in some way or other, he is doing more good than evil. But the thoughts came to her uninvited, came in crowds during the day, and especially whenever she had written home, which she often did. When her thoughts became too much for her she went out and drank.

One night she was walking the streets after despatching home a letter enclosing a little money. It was eleven o'clock. The people were coming out of the theatres in crowds and she looked on at them. Some of them returned

her look and that of women like her – that look of pas-
sion and desire that works destruction, that sets country
against country, and that has furnished materials to poets
and novelists from the time of Troy down to the present
day.

In a few minutes she saw a man just in front of her
accompanied by his wife. He looked at her and Nora at
him without knowing why. Then they recognised each
other. It was John Mat's son, now a doctor in London.
Nora turned away immediately, but she heard him tell
his wife to go into a restaurant just at hand and that he
would follow her in a moment.

On hearing this Nora walked away briskly. He followed her. She accelerated her pace, and he did the same.
She only wanted to elude him. She was now running, and
he ran after her. She was a good bit in front, and she
raced up one street and down another. She thought every
second that he was at her heels, she was terrified lest he
should overtake her, lest the people at home, lest everybody, should get to know of her way of living.

Right in front of her stood a chapel – a little chapel
that was open that night in honour of some feast. There
lay a way of escape from the man who was following her,
from the man whom she had once loved, but who had
deceived her. She had no thought of entering the chapel,
but enter it she did.

Everything she saw at first seemed strange to her it was
so long since she had been in a church. Her youth came
back to her. She was again in the church at Rosdaloch.
There was a statue of the Blessed Virgin in a corner before which burned a red light. She went over to the corner and threw herself on her knees before the statue. She
embraced its feet. She swayed to and fro in agony of mind.
Her fine feathered hat slipped to the back of her head.

Her fine ribbons were wet, dirty and stained with mud. She was praying aloud to God and the Blessed Virgin – prayer after prayer – and she said in a loud, earnest voice –

'Holy Mary! Mother of God! pray for us sinners now and at the hour of our death. Amen.'

An old priest who had heard her praying came up behind her. He spoke to her gently and kindly. She answered him, and he took her aside. He questioned her and she told him her whole story, concealing nothing. She showed him the letters from her father. He questioned her further.

'Yes; she was willing to return home. It was she who had sent the money home with which the old man had bought the fishing boat. Indeed they had no suspicion at all of the kind of life she was leading in London.'

'And did your father not ask you why you did not go to your sister at first?'

'He did, but I told him that the work was better in London.'

Question and answer continued for some time. He found her good lodgings for the night and told her to write home saying that she was thinking of going back. He said he would call upon her next day and that she could go to confession.

The same night, before retiring, he wrote a long letter to the parish priest of Rosdaloch, acquainting him of the whole matter and requesting him to look after the young woman on her return home.

She remained for another month in London. The old priest thought it was best to do so. When the month was up she set out for home.

They were expecting her at home. Everyone was saying that she had done better than any other girl who had left Rosdaloch. Nobody had sent home so much money as she had.

'It's a great relief of mind to you, Marcus!' said John the smith, as he was shoeing a horse of Marcus's at the forge on the day of the expected arrival home, 'that she is coming home at last, for you haven't a soul to leave the farm to.'

'You may say so,' answered Marcus, 'and I'm a good age now too.'

He had the horse and car ready to go to meet her at the station.

'They used to say,' he exclaimed proudly, as he put the horse under the car, 'that the other two never did any good. That's true, maybe, but you couldn't believe the help she has been to me. Look at that fine big boat that's going fishing to-night. I couldn't have bought that but for her.'

'You are only saying what is true,' said an old man, who was giving him a hand at yoking the horse. 'But listen,' he continued in a guarded tone, 'did she tell you that our James met her anywhere over there?'

'I asked her about him, but she hadn't seen him.'

'Look at that, now! And I haven't heard from him for six months.'

Marcus set off. He had not been so lighthearted for a long time, as he was on his way to the station. If his sons had turned out badly, in any case his daughter had been splendid. She was an example to the whole parish. Now they would not have it to say that, in the end, he would have to sell the land. He would keep Nora at home. He would get her married. He would get her a quiet steady man.

As he was thus thinking, the train steamed slowly into the station. Nora jumped out. How warmly he welcomed her! And she got even a finer welcome, if that were possible, from her mother at home.

But how thin and tired she looked! What had happened to her? Had she had too much to do? Her native air and the home atmosphere would soon, however, make her all right. She would soon lose her pale cheeks if she stayed with them and followed their advice.

'And the first bit of advice I'd give you is to eat up that plate of meat and cabbage, for I suppose you hadn't a chance of eating a decent meal in the big city,' said the old woman, smiling.

But Nora could not eat. She had completely lost her appetite. She said she was thoroughly upset by the long journey. She would go to her room and undress. She would lie down and rest and presently she might be able to eat something.

'Or maybe you'd like a cup of tea first,' said her mother, when she had retired.

'I would,' answered Nora. 'Perhaps it would do me good.'

When the neighbours came in, the same night, to welcome her back she was not to be seen. They were told that she was so tired and weary after the journey that she had to go to bed, but that they would all see her on the next day. Nora, in her own room, heard their inquiries, and she prayed to God and the Blessed Virgin to make her good and to give her strength to remain so for the future.

5

It was astonishing how Nora worked after her return home. In the same girl, who was called Little Marcus's

Nora in Rosdaloch, there were in reality two persons –
one the quiet young girl who had spent some time in England making money to send it home, and the other a woman – unrecognisable at home – whom life had dealt with
cruelly in a strange city. And even as she seemed to be
two different women, so she seemed to have two personalities and two modes of thought. She had the feelings
of the woman who had led a bad life in London, and she
felt like the girl who had never left her native parish.

The two personalities were for ever at war within her.
The woman who had drunk the bitter cup of life to the
dregs stood opposed to the woman who had never left
home and who desired only to stay there quietly and con-
tentedly. It was a fierce conflict. She felt at times that
the old evil life was re-asserting itself and at such moments she would be seen going to the church – the neighbours, all the while, exclaiming that they had never seen
a young woman so pious, devout and exemplary.

About this time a pattern took place in a neighbouring
village. A great crowd from Rosdaloch attended. Some
walked, some rode, and some crossed the bay in boats.
Some went to sell cattle, some to visit the holy well, and
some went with no special object in view.

Nora was one of those who had no special aim in going. She walked about the fair looking at the cattle that
were being sold, recognising old acquaintances here and
there and making inquiries about others who had left the
district subsequent to her going to London. She looked
extremely well. She wore a white cotton frock very fine
and very costly which she had brought back from England. Her dress was faced with black satin and her toilet-
te was completed with a hat trimmed with feathers. She
had never, for a long time, been so merry and bright.

It was a scorching day. The sun beat down mercilessly.

The heat would have been unbearable were it not for a gentle breeze that blew in, at intervals, from the bay. Nora was exhausted after the day. She caught the sound of a fiddle near at hand – soft, sweet music. The fiddler was sitting at the opening of a tent. His head swayed from side to side; his eyes were closed; and the tranquil and happy look on his face seemed to show that he had never experienced pain or worry and would never know them.

Nora entered and sat on a bench just inside listening to the music. She was dead beat. If she only had something to drink, she thought. The conflict was started again. She was about to leave the tent when a young man from Rosdaloch came up and asked her to join him in a drink.

'The day is so hot and it won't do you a bit of harm. Anything you like,' he said.

She accepted a glass from him.

He who has once been addicted to drink and who has been deprived of it for a while will, if he tastes it once, take a second glass and a third, yea! a ninth, for the old craving will have been revived.

So it was with Nora. She drank a second glass and a third. It soon went to her head. She became boisterous and began to dance. She soon had to stop, however, for her head was in a whirl and she was tottering on her feet. She got out with difficulty, but she had not gone far when she collapsed in a ditch.

It was long after dark when her father found her there, and, lifting her into the car, he drove her home.

On the next morning the same car stood outside the door.

'If these are the ways you have learned in England,' the father said in a bitter tone, 'you must go back and practise them there.'

Father and daughter drove off to the railway station.

On the evening of the same day that Nora had been sent away, if you had been at the quay at Rosdaloch, you would have seen an old man busy with a fishing-boat. He had a pot of tar and was obliterating the name on the boat. It was his daughter's name, but though he blotted it out from the side of the boat, he could not efface it from his heart.

Disillusioned

A clock was heard striking in the Mercy Convent, Magheraross, although there might have been only one who
heard it. Even if another girl in the place heard the twelve
strokes, she did not pay the same heed to them as did Peggy Griffin. She heard the clock as she was trying to read
by the feeble light of a street lamp that stood outside the
dormitory window. She thought at first that it was only
eleven o'clock, but when she heard midnight sounding
she began to fear that she might not get sufficient sleep
and that she might not succeed at her examination the
next day. The fact that she was breaking the school rules
did not ruffle her one whit. Had not Sister Mary Alacoque
been asleep for the past two hours, and was she not determined to gain first place at the examination?

As, however, it was really so late she closed her book
and thrust it under her pillow. She pulled the blankets
up round her shoulders, closed her eyes, and seemed to
fall into a sound sleep with her thick brown hair falling
over the pillow. She did not sleep, however, and in a few
minutes she raised her head and took up the book, but
not to read. She took a Christmas card out of the book
and looked at it as if she were reading it. She was not
reading it, for she already knew by heart the words written on it. If she kissed the card and if a tear came to her
grey eye we will pass it over without comment here. If
she did, it is certain that she thought that every one of the
twelve girls in the dormitory with her was asleep.

When she awoke in the morning the examination was
not the first thing she thought of. She was to leave for

home that afternoon, and her aunt would be delighted to see her after being away from home for three months. Every night before settling down to sleep she drew her pen through the date just passed in the little calendar that was fixed to her desk, and she made believe that it was her affection for her aunt that made her glad that the day was over. And why should she not be light-hearted on this blessed morning? Had not the great day arrived? Would she not be with her aunt before sunset? If Peggy had another reason to be pleased she concealed it from herself. She hoped to meet often during the holidays the sender of the Christmas card that she had se-cretly kissed – if indeed she had kissed it. No sensible girl, however, in her early teens would allow herself to think that she cared so much for a man who was twice her age, and Peggy was a rock of sense.

It was twenty long miles from Magheraross to Derry-navea, where Peggy and her aunt lived, and the night was falling as the car passed the post office near Derrynavea. Not far from the post office there is a dip in the road and bushes grow at each side. The post reaches Derry-navea late in the evening, and scarcely an evening passed that a tall, graceful young man, with a soldierly bearing, might not be seen walking away from the post office with a paper or two under his arm. He often rested at the dip in the road, when the weather was favourable, reading of the doings of the big world upon which he had turned his back. A person looking down upon him from a height would have thought that he was a priest or brother in religion, for the people in Derrynavea did not wear black clothes. However wide was your knowledge of the ways of the world and its people, and of the manner of dress of each race and occupation, you could not tell what race he belonged to or what occupation he followed by merely looking at him. You would immediately recognise that he was a man of intelligence; you would realise that he had seen much of the world both bad and good; but when he raised his eyes from the paper as you passed by you might feel that if you carried a secret you must needs tell it to the person who possessed such a pair of eyes.

This is just what poor Peggy thought the first day she met him at his favourite restingplace a year before, but for all the world she would not tell him her secret now. She told the driver to whip up the horse lest the man might be at the dip in the road as she passed and lest she might have to talk to him, or even give him a lift, as he was a next-door neighbour. When, however, he was not to be seen, her heart fell. A feeling of loneliness oppressed her, but she did not analyse the cause of this feeling, even if she understood it. She hardly understood it, for she was only sixteen, and how often does one experience such a feeling at dusk, especially at the commencement of summer.

Dear, dear, Peggy!

Although Peggy's aunt lived alone, save for an old servant-woman, there was always company on the evening that the girl came home from school on her holidays. On that night there was a little party, but only the more important people in the place were invited. Peggy was always much amused at these people, for she was naturally bright and witty, and she often had a quiet smile at her aunt's visitors. On this night, however, it was noticed that she was more thoughtful, and that she talked less than usual. She sat in a little chair at the window idly turning over the pages of a volume of music. She was longing for bedtime and was tired of the party.

She suddenly started, however, at the entrance of a tall, slender man dressed in black. He greeted the company, spoke lowly, and in a very friendly way to the hostess – Peggy's aunt – and was about to sit down on a chair near the piano, when he noticed the girl at the window.

'Hasn't she grown, Brigid?' said he to her aunt. 'She'll have to wear long frocks now and do her hair differently.'

He addressed these remarks to the aunt, but Peggy heard them, and when she saw him coming over to shake hands with her she made up her mind not to speak to him at all. She would show him that she was not to be made fun of, but she forgot her resolution when she saw his hand stretched out to her and his two keen humorous eyes looking through her.

She was so much agitated that the volume of music fell from her lap to the floor, but as she continued to hold the page she happened to be turning that page was torn out of the book. She herself and the tall man stooped at the same moment to take up the book, with the result that both their heads knocked together. This little accident upset her very much.

'Sit down near me, Tom Kane!' said the doctor. 'I want to talk to you about modern Spanish literature.'

The tall man sat near the doctor and they began a learned conversation, but nobody paid the slightest attention to what they said except Peggy. She was near them drinking in every word and eagerly waiting for an opportunity to join in to show Tom Kane that she was no child. She thought of a suitable remark, but when she tried to utter it she lost her nerve. When she was about to make another remark, the doctor interrupted her with some silly remark that made everybody laugh.

Peggy, however, had spirit, and when the laugh was over, she said:

'The doctor's opinion on that subject isn't worth much,

as he can't read Spanish.'

She hardly knew whether she finished the sentence. Her own voice terrified her, and she was sure that she had made a fool of herself. Tom Kane would never think anything of her again. When they laughed at something else that was said, she imagined that they were laughing at her. She wished the ground would open and swallow her. She thought she heard Tom asking her did she speak Spanish, or whether she was learning that beautiful language at school, but she was not certain whether she had heard him aright. She held her head low so that they migt not observe her agitation. Tears welled up in her eyes and she was afraid every moment she would burst out crying, but she succeeded in restraining them.

Luckily enough refreshments were brought in and the guests were too busy for half-an-hour to discuss Spanish literature, or any such subject.

When Peggy had finished her refreshments, she slipped out into the garden.

Tom Kane had a cow sick, and as he was, in consequence unable to spend much time at the party, he said good-bye and withdrew. As he went out the gate, he heard a voice say, 'Mr. Kane, do not think that I am a child, for I am not, and besides, I have a good knowledge of Spanish, and I would prove –'

Kane did not hear what she could prove, as the girl became suddenly bashful, and retreated behind the bushes.

After she came back from the garden, she thought that all present would be curiously looking at her. When they had not noticed her absence at all, she became excited, and, as Tom had gone home, she got very timid. If her condition was noticed at all, it was set down to the long journey she had had.

During the remainder of her holidays, Peggy had a

pleasant time. Every morning on getting up she was anxious lest she should not meet Kane during the course of the day; she thought of all he had said to her at their previous meeting; she thought out things to say to him at their next meeting, all the time being very much afraid that she might not get an opportunity of speaking fully to him. At this time she was seen walking the roads with a book in her hand, but the book was a mere excuse. As a rule she was weaving romantic stories in which herself and Tom Kane figured largely. At one time they were together on an island out at sea. At another time she was being drowned in some big river and he came to her rescue. Anon she saw him riding a fine horse across the broad plains of Argentina. Again he was working in a mine beneath the ground in control of hosts of rough, wild men.

Very rarely, however, was she able to talk to him properly at first, as he usually turned the conversation into remarks of a flattering or jocose nature. If he had known what her real trouble was he might have been more on his guard, but he was quite unconscious of her feelings. He believed that she was merely a child – a very pretty and very interesting child.

About a week after her return from school, she and her aunt paid a visit to the town. She was waiting for her aunt in a room in the hotel and, as pen and paper lay convenient, she began to write a letter. In this letter she said quite a lot that she would never have said if she had had any thought of despatching the letter. When she had it half finished, she was very pleased with what she had written, and she resolved to re-write it and alter the handwriting so that Tom Kane might not recognise it. She was wearing some flowers in her blouse, and as there was no one looking at her, she tied them with a strand of her hair and slipped them into the envelope.

She regretted it when she had posted the letter. If he were to recognise the writing she would be shamed for ever. She wished very much to see him reading the letter. On the next afternoon where was she but concealed behind the bushes beside the road near the post office? Her heart began to beat more rapidly when she saw Tom Kane coming up the road with his letters and papers in his hand. He seemed to be in a thoughtful mood. He was quite near to where the girl lay concealed. He was so near to her that she could see her own letter in his hand. She knew it by its blue envelope, and she was about to emerge from her hiding-place and as kit from him.

She did not stir, however. She saw him read it and she saw him laugh immoderately as he read the silliest bits.

When he had gone she found the flowers on the road. She felt she was lucky that he had not noticed them at all.

2

On account of an accident to his hand, Kane was unable to write, and as he had to reply to some letters he came to his neighbour's house to get them written.

Peggy was the only one at home, and she was delighted to be able to help him. She took up a pen and began to write as he told her. They were seated at either side of the parlour table. He raised his eyes from time to time to see whether his young amanuensis had taken down what he had dictated. Peggy's head was bent over her work as she covered the paper skilfully and rapidly. No sound was heard but the scratching of the pen and the breathing of the girl. The letters to be written were long, and when he looked at her she knew without raising her head that he was scanning her closely. She was upset by the way he looked at her, with the result that she spoiled a sheet of paper. He took up the spoiled sheet and began to read it.

'You are a fine writer, and very smart with your pen, but where have I seen that handwriting before?'

She was in terror lest he was going to recognise her handwriting. How unfortunate it was that she had sent that letter to him! She was about to say that it was not she who had sent the letter, but how would she have known there was such a letter if she herself had not written it?

The poor girl was in a bad state.

'Have you that much down?' said he, as he noticed that her pen had come to a stop.

'Yes,' she answered in a weak voice, as she saw that he was watching her closely.

He commenced dictating again, but stopped in a minute or two. When the girl glanced up, she saw a look of understanding in his eyes, and she was convinced that he was aware of her secret and had known it for a long time. This was not the case, however, and he had suspected nothing until he saw her writing and recognised its similarity to that in the anonymous letter he had received.

Then he began to think of a lot of things he had observed since Peggy's return from school. He put one thing and another together, and it was not surprising that a look of humour came into his eyes. If, however, he was half-laughing, he was also very anxious. He had never looked at her as anything but a child. He thought her a bright and pretty child, and had always been interested in her antics and quaint little ways, but now that he recognised how things were with her, he realised that he should be on his guard, and that he should cure her, if possible.

Peggy, seeing his thoughtful look, understood the reason for it. She threw down her pen with an impatient gesture, and with the words 'finish your letters yourself', she flounced out of the room with tears in her eyes. Before long it was noticed that there was a great change in Peggy's demeanour. She was never in the same place with Kane if she could possibly avoid it. It was noticed, too, that she was becoming very sensible and serious. She did not speak much, but when she did she was worth listening to. If Kane dropped in on a visit and found her alone in the house she made some excuse for going outside. She had to look after the hens or the ducks, to go here, to go there, and if Kane said that nothing would please him better than to help her, she made it clear to him that she preferred to be alone.

She was pleased that she could show Tom that she paid no attention to him and was not interested in his doings, and she was delighted at being able to fool him thoroughly. She was fonder than ever of him, but she gave no sign of it, although she found it hard at times not to tell him all. She kept her own counsel, and she would not have confessed her feelings for anything in the world.

Kane was puzzled, and he came to the conclusion that he had been wrong in his diagnosis of Peggy's complaint. He now thought that it only existed in his imagination. If, he thought, she really cared so much for him, why should she seek so much to avoid him?

He had been anxious and worried at the thought that she had felt so deeply about him, as it was bad for a highly strung girl like her. Was it not a great blessing that she had been cured? It was a great relief to him at any rate, and he now thought that it would, in the circumstances, be no harm to be kind and friendly to her as in the past.

He dropped in often when Peggy was alone, and they

chatted in a very friendly way. At first the girl thought of avoiding him, but she was so interested in his conversation that she could not leave. She was a good listener, and there was very little that he said that she did not remember. He told her of his life beyond the seas, and how interested she was in that life! He spoke of the wonders he had seen, of the queer, extraordinary people he had met in foreign countries, of the work he had done there, of the books he had read until the girl's heart filled with delight. Never, to her thinking, was conversation so full of understanding, and intelligence and vigour. Surely he would not speak to her in that way unless he had a very high regard for her! Not in that manner would he speak to a child! She took comfort to her heart that the man she loved was becoming more intimate with her.

She became depressed presently when her aunt came in, and when Tom turned to talk to her, disregarding Peggy. Nothing pained her so much as this lack of attention. She would have been jealous of her aunt if the aunt had been a little younger, for she thought that no man could be in love with her aunt considering her age. Tom was the soul of courtesy, and he could not help talking to her aunt in a friendly way, especially in her own house. Of course he would have preferred that she was not present.

'She is getting near forty,' said Peggy to herself. 'See how worn she is; look at her lined forehead; and she is getting gray, too.'

Peggy's judgment was astray, however. Her aunt was not more than thirty-four, and even if her forehead was wrinkled and she was getting grey after all she had seen and suffered before obtaining her fine farm, Tom Kane loved her better than any woman he had ever met.

Peggy knew nothing of this. She fondly believed that he liked her better than any woman in the place, otherwise why should he spend so much time in her company? Alas! she totally misunderstood the situation.

'It is lovely to see a plant growing ripe under the summer sun,' said Tom to himself, 'but it is lovelier to see the heart and soul of a maiden advancing in growth from day to day,' and he continued his visits and his talks, not believing that he was doing any harm.

After all, Peggy was merely a child. One day on returning after half-an-hour's talk with Tom at the crossroads, she came across a number of children. They were pretending to be cows, and were having splendid fun. Peggy watched them for some time, and as she saw that they were not playing the game properly, she started to show them how it should be played. To be a proper cow, she had to go on all fours, crying out 'moo, moo!' She took as much delight in the game as any of the children, but she suddenly got up when she noticed that Tom Kane was an interested spectator.

A young woman like her playing with schoolchildren, with him looking on! She was terribly ashamed. She resolved to tell him that it was only a game, and that she was only instructing them how to play, but she could not find her tongue.

'Oh, don't mind me,' said he, with laughter in his eyes, 'I love to see children making fun.'

'But I'm not a chid,' replied Peggy, turning away indignantly to hide her tears.

She would not have wished for anything that he should see her in such an attitude. What could a man think of her to be occupied in such a way? It was a horrible mischance that he had so seen her. She remained at home disconsolate until nightfall.

At this time the hens were laying outside, and Peggy's aunt had much-ado in collecting the eggs. The hens wandered a good distance from the house, and she went on an old bicycle in search of them. On the day in question, she was out in quest of eggs, and, after Peggy had left Kane, he observed her aunt coming down the road on her bicycle with an old straw hat on and her basket fastened to the handle-bar. He knew well where she was going. He had been cutting bushes with a saw when he encountered Peggy, and he still had the saw in hand. He made off through the stubbles with a great appearance of work. At intervals he saw the old straw hat bobbing up and down over the hedge. He reached one of his own fields which was separated by a hedge from the land of the woman he was in love with, and he began to cut away the bushes in the hedge. He had made great havoc when the woman with the old straw hat arrived on the scene in search of her eggs. She saw the damage that had been done to the hedge, but she did not at first observe the perpetrator. When she caught sight of Tom as he worked at topspeed with his saw, she thought the poor man had lost his senses.

'What's the matter with you?' she said, 'you have ruined the hedge.'

He raised his head. Up to then he had not pretended to see her at all.

'Is it you, Brigid?' Come here and help me. This is very hard work,' he said.

'Help you! Are you mad?' she answered.

'I am not. We don't want a hedge here any more. We are going to have one big farm.'

They returned home together, and they found Peggy at the house. Tea was made, and they were all enjoying it when Tom put his hand on the girl's head, and said:

'We are soon going to have a wedding here, Peggy!'

Peggy started. At first she thought that he was asking

for her hand, and she was much disappointed that he had not left the proposal for an occasion when she was alone with him. She blushed, and was thinking of making a suitable reply when her aunt said:

'Yes, Peggy dear, the match is made. We are to be married in a month!'

Poor Peggy nearly swooned away on hearing these words. She heard no more of what they said. When tea was over she stole away into the garden and spent a great portion of the night there, well nigh broken-hearted.

Sometime afterwards Peggy was received in the Mercy Convent, Magheraross. The papers contained a long account of the reception, and mentioned that amongst those present were Mr. Thomas Kane and his wife. Neither of them knew what had induced Peggy to enter, and they suspect that she will not remain long there.

The Woman on whom God laid His Hand

There wasn't a finer little boat in Galway Bay than the *Cailin Beag Donn,* and, as the shopkeeper who owned her was about to sell her, Padraic O'Nea thought that the boat would be a nice dowry for his daugther, if he could get it reasonably cheap. But Antony O'Malley, the young woman's intended husband, thought that they should try the boat before purchasing to see whether she was nearly as good as her reputation. The old man agreed that it was a good idea and so he, his son James, and O'Malley set out for a night's fishing to test the qualities of the boat.

Kate, the engaged girl, accompanied her people to the quay to see them off, and she remained a good while on the rising ground looking at the fishing fleet sailing out of the bay before the wind. It was late in the evening when she returned home and her mother had the supper ready. The table was laid, the cake was cooling on the window-sill, and the kettle was singing pleasantly. The two women sat down, and from time to time they looked through the window at the boats, which looked like a community of nuns taking the air in a convent garden.

It was getting very calm. The birds, which had been singing merrily an hour before, were getting listless. It seemed that the denizens of the air were getting tired of their melody, and that they would never practice it again. Birds and beasts were getting drowsy, but the young woman remained at the window until the boats disappeared from sight in the darkness and a bright star arose in the western sky.

The old woman at the fire heaved a sigh.

'What is the matter with you, mother?' said Kate, getting up and going over to her.

'I shall be very lonely without you, dear!'

'Won't you have my father and James, too?'

'James won't stay long. Young people now want only to go away.'

'But, mother, didn't you often make us laugh by telling us how you went off with my father against the wishes of your people?' said Kate, in order to cheer up her mother.

'And look at the life I've spent since.'

Her mother did not often complain, and it disturbed the young woman to find that it was about such things she was thinking. She knew well that her mother's people had been so much opposed to the marriage, that they had never spoken to her since. Her mother had been a well-brought-up and well-educated girl, but she accepted the life her husband was able to give her.

'But I'm not running away from you,' said Kate. 'You'll see me often. Sure I won't be more than twenty miles away.'

'I know that, treasure!' said her mother, 'but, for some time now, I've been thinking that my father's curse has followed me. See how they've all left me, and now you are going. It seems to me that the reason why they all left me was that I am a little bit queer now and again. Isn't there a saying 'even to the seventh generation'?'

Kate took her mother's hand and stroked it affectionately. She knew well what was in her mother's thoughts. She was aware that in nearly every generation of her mother's people there had been someone who was a little bit queer – so queer, indeed, that some of them had to be placed under restraint. The neighbours, however, did not know this. Her mother had come from another country, and if one or two people had heard the story, no one had exact particulars.

'You shouldn't say that,' said Kate, in an anxious tone.

'But it's true, Kate!' answered the old woman.

The night fell, and Kate lit the lamp and drew the blind. Three visitors came in – three that are not often seen. They were Anxiety, Terror, and Hope. The old woman at the fire saw them, and she surprised her daughter by making some apparently inconsequent remarks. Kate thought that her mother was getting queerer every day.

'The wind is rising, and it's very dangerous at sea to-night,' said the old woman, speaking with the tone of Anxiety.

The daughter pulled up the blind. The moon was up and the sea was very calm – so calm that it seemed that never again would it drown anybody.

'Look out, mother! There isn't a ripple. It's sleepy you are.'

The boat was not expected back until the early morning.

'I'll stay here till morning,' said the old woman, in a brooding tone. 'What a lot of people have been drowned here in my time! Pat's Paddy and his people were drowned last year on a moonlight night just like this; and little Peg's Michael and his sister this time two years, and two or three years ago the people of the Island were drowned.'

The mother went on muttering at the fire, but her remarks did not worry Kate. There were not in the whole bay two finer boatmen than her father and O'Malley.

'Come over here!' said the old woman, suddenly.

She went over, and the old woman seized her two hands and gazed into her eyes.

'Kate! Tell me the truth,' she said. 'If one or two of the boat's crew is to be drowned to-night, who would you wish to be saved?'

'For God's sake, mother, don't talk like that,' answered

Kate, with a shiver, and she freed herself from her mother's grasp. The women sat by the fire, one on each side. The old woman dropped off asleep, and so did Kate. It was dawn when both were awakened suddenly. Something heavy struck the closed door. The women looked at each other.

'Open the door,' said the old woman quietly, 'until we see which of them has been saved.'

She had, however, to open the door herself, Kate was so terrified, and who should fall inwards in a heap on the floor but O'Malley, soaked with wet and with a look of terror in his eyes.

He was just able to tell the women what had happened. The boat had been wrecked at Carrigalolish. He had succeeded in bringing the old man to land, but life was extinct. The young lad had an oar, but it was not known what had happened to him.

'Let us look for the bodies,' said the old woman, going out.

The boy's body was never found. The beach was searched, from Loop Head right in to Galway, but there was no trace of him. The father was waked, but his wife never shed a tear. At intervals she would be seen in a corner with one of the neighbouring women, talking to her, and if you listened carefully you would hear what she said.

'This drowning is some of the old curse,' she would say. 'How could I cry? Isn't my heart too full? I always knew that he would be drowned some day.'

She would go to the room where the body lay and when she was alone in the room, she spoke to her husband.

'You often laughed at the curse, Patrick!' she said to the corpse, 'but if you are together now, tell my father to lift the curse off me. Will you tell him now, Patrick? I was always fond of you – from the first day I saw you – of your fine head and your sunny face!'

She ceased when a neighbour came into the room, but when the neighbour began to sympathise with her she only said:

'Say no more, now. This drowning is part of my father's curse. It was destined for us from the beginning. Kate is going away, too. Soon I shall be as lonely as I was at first.'

She had to be sent off to rest before daybreak.

After her husband's funeral she became queerer than ever. She would get up at night unknown to Kate and slip out and walk up and down the seashore looking for her son. She was often seen walking at night on the strand – her hair floating in the wind and only a nightdress on – moving along alone, searching every hollow and knocking her feet against the sharp stones. Most frequently she spoke nonsensically, but at times she chanted verses. She sang one that was never heard from anyone but her.

She would say –

> 'I walk about at night
> In rain and before the wind
> Seeking my son, my treasure,
> Where have you gone, Jimmy?'

Then another thought would strike her, and she would say:

> 'But when the Infant Jesus
> Lay at the foot of the Cross,
> You were there, O Mary!
> And He was on your knee.'

And she would say that her sorrow and grief were far greater than that of Mary's as her son's body had not been given back to her after the crucifixion.

> 'Where have you gone from me, Jimmy?
> Why are you not on my knee?'

she would say.

People who heard her talking in this manner tried to take her home. Sometimes they succeeded, but, other times, they did not, and Kate had to go out to her.

She kept up this search and walking by night until Kate had to sleep in the same bed with her. Even then Kate frequently awoke, and, finding her mother gone, had to go out in search of her.

She became worse from day to day. She lost her memory. Her mind was almost a complete blank as far as everything that had happened since her marriage – thirty years ago – was concerned. If her husband was mentioned, she said she had no husband, but that she soon would have one in spite of her people. If anything about her family was said to her, she would say that she had no family. How could she have one when she was not yet married? But she could tell accurately everything about her early youth. She spoke about it to Kate, believing her to be her sister, her young sister of whom she was fondest, and poor Kate had to listen and keep her in talk until it was far into the night and her heart was breaking.

She spoke of her father oftenest. She would tell her supposed sister of what he had said about the man whom she loved, of how they had met at the fair, of how he had abused the young man, and of how the young man had struck him.

'And wasn't he right?' she would say, 'as he had called

him a rotten beggar? But he will come for me yet and I'll run away with him in spite of them all, and you will help me, Brigid, will you not?'

Poor Kate was an object of pity as she listened to her mother speaking gaily and romantically of her father who had been drowned – the old woman believing that she was still young and about to marry him.

She had not a bad attack very often, however. She was very bad once a month or so. If one of her bad days came, and Kate did not happen to be near her, she would put on her wedding dress, which she had laid by in a trunk, and she would dress up like a young woman of thirty years back.

If anyone met her she would say that she had run away from her father, that she was dressed up for the man whom she loved and that they would be united before the morrow morning.

It was a queer and sad sight to see the old woman, on whom God had laid His hand, walking the roads with her bright ribbons and her lovely bits of lace floating in the wind, but it was a far sadder sight to see the young woman searching for her and inquiring about her anxiously.

But there was no evil in the old woman on whom God had laid His hand. She was gentle towards everyone.

The neighbours pitied them both. As for the old woman, she had always been a bit queer ever since she came to the place, but they did not realise that her mind had completely gone, and they did not know that the same ailment which had affected many of her people had now attacked her. The neighbours could not be aware of all this, as they knew very little about the people to whom she belonged, and if she was now a little queerer than before, it was no wonder, considering all she had suffered, the creature!

Kate, however, recognised the disease, but she kept her knowledge from everybody. She did not tell it even to O'Malley, and she soon regretted her reticence with him. At first she had no idea of concealing it from him, but one day, when they were talking, he asked her did she think it was that disease her mother had and she answered 'No.' At the time she really did not think so, and when she finally was convinced of her mother's condition, she did not tell him, as she would have had to tell him all. She would have had to tell him all about her people, of her two uncles in the asylum and of the aunt who, for twenty years, could never go out of the house alone. She often spoke to her mother about the matter, and, oftener still, she thought over it and came to think that the young man knew as much about it as she did herself. What would he say to her? The match would be broken off, and how she loved him! And how did she know what change might take place? When they were married she would tell him everything, bit by bit. He would have become accustomed to the ways of the woman on whom God had laid His hand. He would pity her and her people when he understood. In one way or another she thought it better to defer telling him.

About this time it occurred to Kate that it would be good for the patient if she were to go away for a long time to some place away from the sea. The rock on which the boat had been wrecked was visible at low tide, and her mother could see it from her own house. Would it not be a good thing if she went to live far from the sight of that accursed rock?

Away in the County Mayo lived her elder married sister, and the young woman thought it well to pay her a visit. They were not as friendly as two sisters ought to be, and when, after her long journey, Kate arrived at the house she received but a poor welcome.

The sister and her husband kept a public-house, and as they were better off than the people at home, the sister had an idea that Kate had come to look for assistance – a thing that had happened on a previous occasion. She would not have come so far without an invitation unless that were the case.

Kate's brother-in-law was serving in the shop and the two sisters found themselves alone, but as there was a small window between the room in which they sat and the shop, they could hear distinctly the voices of the men who were drinking.

'Well, Kate, and how is mother?' asked the sister.

'Poorly – very poorly, Mary!'

The married sister was knitting, but she took her eyes off her work from time to time, and affection and meanness could be seen struggling in her eyes.

'Is she worse?'

'Yes, much worse.'

'Did she do anything queer lately, Kate?'

'She does something queer every day in the year, Mary!'

Both kept silent for a while. The singing of a young man who was tipsy came from the shop.

'Every day I get up I am afraid of my life that she'll do something dreadful,' said Kate. 'She recognises me only occasionally now. She thinks I am her sister, that I am Brigid O'Donnell.'

'The Lord save us! And she hasn't seen Brigid for thirty-two years since she married father!'

The proprietor's voice, speaking loudly to the singer, came to their ears.

'And Brigid and her husband are becoming very friendly to us,' said the married sister after deliberation. 'They were here the day before yesterday, and they had tea with us in a nice and friendly way, and the captain said that he had never, except once in India, tasted such tea.'

'Bad luck to Brigid and the captain, too!' said Kate impatiently; 'it's not to talk about them that I came on this journey.'

An aunt of theirs who was married to a captain in the army was the subject of their talk. This couple never used the words 'aunt' or 'uncle' for the wife's people. They were snobs, and they would have nothing to do with the poor sister or her children. Neither of them had come even to the funeral.

'Aren't you very impatient?' said the married sister; 'but is she bad every day?'

'No. Sometimes she is quite herself, but she is a more pitiful sight then than at other times.'

Kate stood up and her voice was sharp and bitter.

'Mary!' she said, 'my heart is breaking. No one but God knows what I have suffered for the past year. I am there in the kitchen with her and she is sitting at the window looking out at the sea with such grief in her face as you never saw. She wants to go away, but she cannot. Her eyes are glued to the place where that accursed rock is. And when the tide goes out, she stays there at the window until the rock is visible. When she sees the rock rising out of the sea according as the tide ebbs, she talks nonsensically to herself until sense and memory leave her. It would be a great blessing from God if she could get away from that awful place for a long time. I'm certain, Mary, that she would be glad to pay you a long visit here.'

She paused to hear what her sister would say.

'Seven and six,' said the proprietor in the shop. 'Take it or leave it.'

The married sister kept silent for a long time. The stocking she had been knitting was on the table in front of her with her spectacles beside it. At last she began to explain to Kate why she could not undertake to look after her mother. Even as it was, the house was too small for them; there was no room for her; they would have to get her an attendant, and money was scarce enough, as a lot was owing to them; they had a large family and an addition was expected shortly; they had to send Tommy to school somewhere, and that would mean another £30 a year.

She spoke on in a similar strain, but Kate was losing all patience.

'And I suppose, Mary, you'd be ashamed of having such a person in the house with you,' said Kate, sarcastically. 'Wouldn't everyone know?'

The other woman stood up quite angry.

'Yes, people here would know it,' she said, 'but O'Malley, who is going to marry you, wouldn't know. To hide it from him you thought of removing your poor mother.'

'No!'

'Yes, I say, for fear he wouldn't marry you, if he knew of the terrible affliction that has followed our people.'

'You lie!'

'And you are a worse liar to say that you have come here for your mother's good.'

The hard and bitter words passed from mouth to mouth, wounding both as it were, with sharp and poisoned knives, and finally Kate left the house vowing vengeance.

Kate had gone off with hatred of her sister in her heart. She made for the railway station, but as the last train had gone, she had to stop in the town till morning. She put up in a hotel near the railway, and as long as she lived she remembered that hotel and the night she spent there.

She did not sleep a wink, but lay in her clothes prone on the bed. She had undertaken that journey for her mother's good, or at least she believed that she had done so. But, on thinking it over during the night, she half-suspected that perhaps her sister had been partly right. Would she have thought at all of bettering her mother if O'Malley were not coming to live with them? Would he not be in and out every hour of the day? Wouldn't he soon notice what was wrong with her mother? And when he would come to hear the terrible news about some of her mother's people, what would he do when she had concealed the whole thing from him? Would he not hate her? And how he told everything to her!

So heavy was the wretched girl's heart, that she imagined that these thoughts were the real motive of her journey. It seemed to her that she had some bad blood. No woman, she had ever known, would do such a thing. To send her poor mother away from her, and all for a man!

When morning came, she no longer remembered the rock on which her relatives were wrecked, nor the sea on which her mother looked in her saner moments, nor the terrible grief visible in the eyes of that mother, nor her own pity, nor the love they had for each other. The heavy word that had been spoken to her stuck in her heart. She thought she was the worst woman ever born.

But he who does penance for his evil deeds can get pardon from God and from man. She would do penance. She would never marry. She would stay at home minding her mother and waiting upon her to the day of her death. Next day, when she would see O'Malley, she would tell him the whole truth. He would hate her surely, but in time perhaps he would forgive her for having deceived him, and in a couple of years or so would he not come back as her friend in another way?

Young and comely as she was, she had a heart as heavy as lead as she sat alone in the carriage when the train departed. She realised that day why, in the prayer of the Church, this lovely world is called a valley of tears.

On reaching her own town, she saw a small crowd outside the house of John O'Neill, the magistrate. There was a car in the street, with a policeman holding the horse. As she passed the house, she noticed that they all looked sharply at her, and that some of them apparently wished to speak to her, but hesitated to do so.

She had not gone far when she was called back, and, turning, she entered the house. She found her mother there with her wedding dress on, but how wet and dirty! The ribbons and lace, which once were white, hung down from her disordered garment. She was sitting on a chair singing a love long.

O'Malley was present, and he explained matters to Kate. He said that her mother had got a seizure that morning, that she had escaped from the old woman who was minding her, and that she had injured one of the neighbours – a woman, who was taking her home. They were going to commit her to the asylum.

Kate spoke to her, but she did not recognise her. She rambled in her speech, and said she was grateful to those gentlemen – meaning the police – and was thankful to them, as they were about to take her to the man she loved.

But she recognised Kate when she was placed on the car, or she thought she was her sister.

'I always trusted you,' she said, 'but you tried to keep me from him like the rest. But you couldn't. These gentlemen came to my help. He sent them to me.'

'O youth of the grey eyes
To whom I gave my hearts's love.'

were the last words that Kate heard from her as the car
went down the road.

Kate and O'Malley went on towards the house. They
had two-and-a-half miles to walk, but neither of them
spoke a word until they were at the quay almost. It was
a lovely evening and the birds were singing in the trees.
The fishing fleet was leaving the harbour in full sail. If,
on an evening like this, there is sorrow and heartbreak
in the world, it is surely of man's doing and not God's
will.

O'Malley wished to say something to the girl whom
he loved, but what could he say?

At last he had to speak.

'Have courage, dear,' he said.

'I will.'

'God has laid a heavy hand on her,' he said.

'But He has laid a heavier hand on those she left behind,' said she, 'but we accept it as God's will.'

There is a rock near the quay which is called 'The
Big Chair,' and as they were passing the rock, she said:

'Let us sit here for a little, Antony!'.

They sat down. He held her hand and she gazed at the
sea, deep in thought.

'For two years I have often thought,' she said, almost
to herself it seemed, 'I have often thought, when she
would have one of her bad attacks, that a person gains
nothing by having the use of his reason and understanding, and that he is better for the loss of reason. She has
a light and joyful heart to-night, but my heart is as black
as coal and as heavy as lead.'

The young man did not understand her fully.

'It is reason that has ruined our lives,' she said.

'But listen, Kate dear!' he said. 'Our lives have not been been in store for us both together, with God's help.'

'No. I will never marry.'

'You will never marry – why?'

'I deceived you, Antony! I never told you what ailed my mother.'

'But I knew it myself. A thing like that is not to be talked about,' said the young man, in a surprised tone.

'And I concealed from you the condition of my mother's people. I never told you that she has two brothers in the asylum and a sister not much better than they.'

'What in the world is wrong with you, Kate?' he said. 'Have I not known that for years?'

The girl was surprised, but she asked him no question. She burst into tears.

The sun was setting when they parted.

'It's no use in your talking to me: I will never marry,' were the last words she said to him that evening.

And she never married. O'Malley came often to ask her, but she never gave in. She is still living in the cottage near the quay, and often she can be seen at the little window looking out on the sea and on the rock where her people were wrecked, and waiting for the day when she will be in heaven with her mother, or in the asylum.

First published in the Netherlands